Macmillan Advanced Readers Series

The Tell-Tale Heart and other stories

by
EDGAR ALLAN POE
ROBERT GRAVES
H. G. WELLS
JOHN GALSWORTHY
E. F. BENSON
JOHN WYNDHAM
ROALD DAHL
ALGERNON BLACKWOOD

Edited with Introduction by
Keith Jones
General Editors: Dr C. A. Bitter
Dr C. Swatridge

MACMILLAN

First published 1986

Published by *Macmillan Publishers Ltd*
London and Basingstoke
Associated companies and representatives in Accra,
Auckland, Delhi, Dublin, Gaborone, Hamburg, Harare,
Hong Kong, Kuala Lumpur, Lagos, Manzini, Melbourne,
Mexico City, Nairobi, New York, Singapore, Tokyo

Printed in Hong Kong

The Tell-tale heart and other stories.—
(Macmillan advanced readers series)
1. English language—Text-books for
foreign speakers   2. Readers—1950–
I. Jones, Keith
428.6'4   PE1128
ISBN 0-333-42745-9

Contents

Acknowledgements

The publishers wish to thank the following who have kindly given permission for the use of copyright material.

William Heinemann Ltd. for 'Timber' from *Caravan* by John Galsworthy; David Higham Associates Ltd. for 'A Long Spoon' by John Wyndham, published by Michael Joseph Ltd; Murray Pollinger for 'Skin' by Roald Dahl from *Someone Like You* published by Michael Joseph Ltd. and Penguin Books Ltd; A. P. Watt & Son for 'The House With the Brick Kiln' by E. F. Benson, published by permission of the Estate of E. F. Benson, and 'Earth to Earth' from *The Collected Short Stories* by Robert Graves, published by permission of Robert Graves and Cassell & Co. Ltd. and 'The Truth About Pyecraft' from *The Short Stories of H. G. Wells* published by permission of the Estate of H. G. Wells, and 'Running Wolf' by Algernon Blackwood, published by permission of The Public Trustee.

The publishers have made every effort to trace the copyright-holders but if they have inadvertently overlooked any, they will be pleased to make the necessary arrangement at the first opportunity.

Cover photograph: Science Photo Library

iv

Introduction

Thinking about art is asking four questions. What is it about? What happens? How it is shown? What does it mean?

What is it About?
A work of art like the short story is the artist's response to a problem. Different kinds of problems come together as 'Themes'. A theme is a group of related problems. The theme of the macabre is the problem of disorder. Disorder in the mind. Disorder in nature. Disorder in society. 'Madness, Mystery and Murder'.

What Happens?
The short story, like the play and the novel, is cast in the form of a 'Plot'. A plot is not just action. A plot is the relationship between characters and circumstances. A plot is the events that occur in *thought* and *action* when certain *characters* meet in certain *circumstances*. In the plots of the macabre, order breaks down, unexpected events take place, life becomes uncertain, people do not know what to do. Sometimes the effect is wonder, sometimes amusement, but very often the result is panic, horror, terror, violence, death.

How is it shown?
The short story like all art forms uses signs to produce 'Images'. The signs of a short story are phrases and combinations of phrases. The images are *word-paintings* of people and places, are

word-films of actions and reactions, are *word-conjurings* of thoughts and feelings. And the images are placed, like islands in a river, in a stream of narration, of story-telling, of *word-reports* that feed the reader with background information. The images are jewels. The narration is the cloth on which they lie. In the best writing the images come in pairs as 'Metaphors'. To present an image in his plot metaphorically the writer takes a corresponding image from the general world of his experience and links the two:

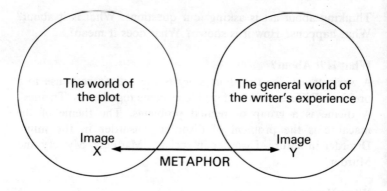

in simile or fuses the two in metaphor. A metaphor is an XY sign, a union of two images and two areas of experience, X is shown as analogous to Y. To present an image of a person deep in thought (X) we can use an image of a person standing in a deep pool of water (Y): the verb 'immerse' carries both images along in a train of associations. A metaphor transports experience from one area of knowledge into another. But the writer not only *reveals* through image as metaphor, he also *suggests,* hints, half-states, partly presents, through 'Image as Symbol'.

A symbol is an image that recurs, that repeats itself, that grows in meaning as the plot unfolds. *Earth to Earth* has a powerful example in the image of the compost heap. Just as love helps a woman to conceive so the compost heap helps the soil produce better and bigger crops.

We have the parallel process of:

$$\text{WOMAN} \longrightarrow \text{LOVE} \longrightarrow \text{CHILD}$$
$$\text{GARDEN} \longrightarrow \text{COMPOST} \longrightarrow \text{CROP}$$

In the story a woman who cannot have children turns to her garden. The garden becomes a substitute womb. But it is not what the garden can grow that she gets involved in. It is not the crop that she concentrates on. It is not the end, the goal, but the means. It is the compost heap that obsesses her. What does the compost heap symbolize in the story? The answer is there is no single answer. A symbol is an image that has many correspondences in one experience and different people will find different correspondences. The compost heap swallows up the garden in the story. Passion and obsession swallow up people if they get out of hand, is one crude way of interpreting this. But decide for yourself. A symbol is an equation that everyone has to solve for themselves. A metaphor is an image the author interprets for you. A symbol is an image you have to interpret for yourself.

What Does it Mean?

What does the macabre mean? In the macabre people get damaged. The hero is often the victim. Life is seen through a glass, darkly, bloodily. The macabre is the art form of failure. The failure of imagination and energy to keep in touch with reason and love. The failure of Dr Faustus. The failure of Macbeth.

What the artist does is to produce 'Myths'. He takes some vital philosophical problem like evil, disorder, violence. He reasons it out not through logic or experiment like a scientist but through the creation of a world of characters and circumstances that mimic his understanding of the real world. He talks about that world through a narrator who may also be a character and he presents events from that world, using signs to create images. And the text that results, the marks on paper, add up to a kind of explanation of the problem or conflict he has been exploring. The artist in general is saying, here is an object I have made: a film, a book, a painting: this object is a model of how I see a problem working itself out in life: look in the model, in this little theatre, it might help you understand where we come from, who we are, where we are going. It might help because I, in my imagination, have tried to live in this world myself. My film, my book, my painting is a map of where I've been and a model of what happened there.

The map and the model make up the myth. In the macabre the models are madness, mystery and murder in action and the maps are maps of hell.

Where does Hell come from?

From energy that has nowhere to go? From passion that cannot find an outlet? From loneliness that will murder because that at least is some kind of human contact? From faith in an idea that makes the idea more important than people? From a lust for profit that exploits nature and man alike? From weakness? Greed? Lack of self-honesty?

What is Hell like?

The idea of murder bubbling in a sick mind? The sudden panic as the hero realizes he has made a prison for himself and cannot get out? Knowing the power another person has to destroy you? Reliving the same action leading to destruction year after year, even after death as a ghost? Knowing that what you own is more valued than you are?

Where does Hell take us?

Into consequences we cannot control? Through disorder into sickness and violence? Away from love and reason into passion and profit? Away from dignity and meaning into living out a grotesque sick joke? A spirit that will not be buried? A cynical acceptance that hell is alive and well and living on earth and is better organized by contemporary businessmen than it ever was by the devil himself? A brutal devaluation of life with money as the supreme value?

Can we escape?

How, in fact, does the artist who maps hell for us survive? In *Running Wolf* hell is redeemed, the anger of the old gods is placated and calm and order reappear. Hell is placed in a perspective, understood and overcome. In *Earth to Earth* Hell is in other people. The observer, the narrator, is outraged but he is not dragged down by what he sees. In *Timber,* the ancient Greek view of disorder, of hell, is used to 'explain' where hell comes from. To the Greeks disorder comes from *hubris,* from the arrogance of a belief that man can use, can manipulate, can order the world like a machine. Those guilty of hubris perform certain actions, make certain choices, that bounce back on them and destroy them. Destiny, fate, nemesis, hell, is the return you get on your investment: it is nature talking back to you. We can escape hell through an imaginative understanding of the consequences of our actions. In *The Truth About Pyecraft,* the truth is that Pyecraft does not recognize the truth. Hell is the consequence of self-deception. In *The House With a Brick-Kiln,* hell is in the past but it is not buried. The ghosts continue to enact it. Hell is the absence of peace beyond the grave. Hell is a warning film put on by nature to advertise the consequences of a crime of passion. In *A Long Spoon,* Hell is the sale of the future for the sake of the present. Hell is now gobbling up tomorrow. But through wit and intelligence it is possible to live in it. In *Skin* a man carries another man's vision on his back but does not see it as a commodity. Someone else does. Here Hell is the reward of innocence, of vulnerability, in a society where profit is valued above beauty, money above art.

Keith Jones

The Tell-Tale Heart

EDGAR ALLAN POE

*1809-1849. American poet and writer of stories remarkable
for the originality and ingenuity of their construction. He
was the pioneer of the modern 'horror' story.*

True! — nervous — very, very dreadfully nervous I had been and
am; but why *will* you say that I am mad? The disease had
sharpened my senses — not destroyed — not dulled them. Above
all was the sense of hearing acute. I heard all things in the heaven
and in the earth. I heard many things in hell. How, then, am I mad?
Hearken! and observe how healthily — how calmly I can tell you
the whole story.

It is impossible to say how first the idea entered my brain: but
once conceived, it haunted me day and night. Object there was
none. Passion there was none. I loved the old man. He had never
wronged me. He had never given me insult. For his gold I had no
desire. I think it was his eye! yes, it was this! He had the eye of a
vulture — a pale blue eye, with a film over it. Whenever it fell upon
me, my blood ran cold; and so by degrees — very gradually — I
made up my mind to take the life of the old man, and thus rid
myself of the eye for ever.

Now this is the point. You fancy me mad. Madmen know
nothing. But you should have seen *me*. You should have seen how
wisely I proceeded — with what caution — with what foresight —
with what dissimulation I went to work! I was never kinder to the
old man than during the whole week before I killed him. And every
night, about midnight, I turned the latch of his door and opened it
— oh so gently! And then, when I had made an opening sufficient
for my head, I put in a dark lantern, all closed, closed, so that no
light shone out, and then I thrust in my head. Oh, you would have
laughed to see how cunningly I thrust it in! I moved it slowly —

1

very, very slowly, so that I might not disturb the old man's sleep. It took me an hour to place my whole head within the opening so far that I could see him as he lay upon his bed. Ha! — would a madman have been so wise as this? And then, when my head was well in the room, I undid the lantern cautiously — oh, so cautiously — cautiously (for the hinges creaked) — I undid it just so much that a single thin ray fell upon the vulture eye. And this I did for seven long nights — every night just at midnight — but I found the eye always closed; and so it was impossible to do the work; for it was not the old man who vexed me, but his Evil Eye. And every morning, when the day broke, I went boldly into the chamber, and spoke courageously to him, calling him by name in a hearty tone, and inquiring how he had passed the night. So you see he would have been a very profound old man, indeed, to suspect that every night, just at twelve, I looked in upon him while he slept.

Upon the eighth night I was more than usually cautious in opening the door. A watch's minute hand moves more quickly than did mine. Never before that night, had I *felt* the extent of my own powers — of my sagacity. I could scarcely contain my feelings of triumph. To think that there I was, opening the door, little by little, and he not even to dream of my secret deeds or thoughts. I fairly chuckled at the idea; and perhaps he heard me; for he moved on the bed suddenly, as if startled. Now you may think that I drew back — but no. His room was as black as pitch with the thick darkness (for the shutters were close fastened, through fear of robbers), and so I knew that he could not see the opening of the door, and I kept pushing it on steadily, steadily.

I had my head in, and was about to open the lantern, when my thumb slipped upon the tin fastening, and the old man sprang up in bed, crying out — 'Who's there?'

I kept quite still and said nothing. For a whole hour I did not move a muscle, and in the meantime I did not hear him lie down. He was still sitting up in the bed listening; — just as I have done, night after night, hearkening to the death watches in the wall.

Presently I heard a slight groan, and I knew it was the groan of mortal terror. It was not a groan of pain or of grief — oh, no! — it was the low stifled sound that arises from the bottom of the soul when overcharged with awe. I knew the sound well. Many a night, just at midnight, when all the world slept, it has welled up from my own bosom, deepening, with its dreadful echo, the terrors that distracted me. I say I knew it well. I knew what the old man felt, and pitied him, although I chuckled at heart. I knew that he had been lying awake ever since the first slight noise, when he had turned in the bed. His fears had been ever since growing upon him. He had been trying to fancy them causeless, but could not. He had been saying to himself — 'It is nothing but the wind in the chimney — it is only a mouse crossing the floor,' or 'it is merely a cricket which has made a single chirp.' Yes, he had been trying to comfort himself with these suppositions: but he had found all in vain. *All in vain;* because Death, in approaching him had stalked with his black shadow before him, and enveloped the victim. And it was the mournful influence of the unperceived shadow that caused him to feel — although he neither saw nor heard — to *feel* the presence of my head within the room.

When I had waited a long time, very patiently, without hearing him lie down, I resolved to open a little — very, very little crevice in the lantern. So I opened it — you cannot imagine how stealthily, stealthily — until, at length a single dim ray, like the thread of the spider, shot from out the crevice and fell full upon the vulture eye.

It was open — wide, wide open — and I grew furious as I gazed upon it. I saw it with perfect distinctness — all a dull blue, with a hideous veil over it that chilled the very marrow in my bones; but I could see nothing else of the old man's face or person: for I had directed the ray, as if by instinct, precisely upon the damned spot.

And have I not told you that what you mistake for madness is but over acuteness of the senses? — now, I say, there came to my ears a low, dull, quick sound, such as a watch makes when enveloped in cotton. I knew *that* sound well, too. It was the beating of the old man's heart. It increased my fury, as the beating of a drum stimulates the soldier into courage.

3

But even yet I refrained and kept still. I scarcely breathed. I held the lantern motionless. I tried how steadily I could maintain the ray upon the eye. Meantime the hellish tattoo of the heart increased. It grew quicker and quicker, and louder and louder ever instant. The old man's terror *must* have been extreme! It grew louder, I say, louder every moment! — do you mark me well? I have told you that I am nervous: so I am. And now at the dead hour of the night, amid the dreadful silence of that old house, so strange a noise as this excited me to uncontrollable terror. Yet, for some minutes longer I refrained and stood still. But the beating grew louder, louder! I thought the heart must burst. And now a new anxiety seized me — the sound would be heard by a neighbour! The old man's hour had come! With a loud yell, I threw open the lantern and leaped into the room. He shrieked once — once only. In an instant I dragged him to the floor, and pulled the heavy bed over him. I then smiled gaily, to find the deed so far done. But, for many minutes, the heart beat on with a muffled sound. This, however, did not vex me; it would not be heard through the wall. At length it ceased. The old man was dead. I removed the bed and examined the corpse. Yes, he was stone, stone dead. I placed my hand upon the heart and held it there many minutes. There was no pulsation. He was stone dead. His eye would trouble me no more.

If still you think me mad, you will think so no longer when I describe the wise precautions I took for the concealment of the body. The night waned, and I worked hastily, but in silence. First of all I dismembered the corpse. I cut off the head and the arms and the legs.

I then took up three planks from the flooring of the chamber, and deposited all between the scantlings. I then replaced the boards so cleverly, so cunningly, that no human eye — not even *his* could have detected anything wrong. There was nothing to wash out — no stain of any kind — no blood-spot whatever. I had been too wary for that. A tub had caught all — ha! ha!

When I had made an end of these labours, it was four o'clock

4

— still dark as midnight. As the bell sounded the hour, there came a knocking at the street door. I went down to open it with a light heart, — for what had I *now* to fear? There entered three men, who introduced themselves, with perfect suavity, as officers of the police. A shriek had been heard by a neighbour during the night; suspicion of foul play had been aroused; information had been lodged at the police office, and they (the officers) had been deputed to search the premises.

I smiled, — for *what* had I to fear? I bade the gentlemen welcome. The shriek, I said, was my own in a dream. The old man, I mentioned, was absent in the country. I took my visitors all over the house. I bade them search — search *well*. I led them, at length, to *his* chamber. I showed them his treasures, secure, undisturbed. In the enthusiasm of my confidence, I brought chairs into the room, and desired them *here* to rest from their fatigues, while I myself, in the wild audacity of my perfect triumph, placed my own seat upon the very spot beneath which reposed the corpse of the victim.

The officers were satisfied. My *manner* had convinced them. I was singularly at ease. They sat, and while I answered cheerily, they chatted of familiar things. But, ere long, I felt myself getting pale and wished them gone. My head ached, and I fancied a ringing in my ears: but still they sat and still they chatted. The ringing became more distinct: — it continued and became more distinct: I talked more freely to get rid of the feeling: but it continued and gained definiteness — until, at length, I found that the noise was *not* within my ears.

No doubt I now grew *very* pale; — but I talked more fluently, and with a heightened voice. Yet the sound increased — and what could I do? It was *a low, dull, quick sound — much such a sound as a watch makes when enveloped in cotton*. I gasped for breath — and yet the officers heard it not. I talked more quickly — more vehemently; but the noise steadily increased. I arose and argued about trifles, in a high key and with violent gesticulations; but the noise steadily increased. Why *would* they not be gone? I paced the

5

floor to and fro with heavy strides, as if excited to fury by the observations of the men — but the noise steadily increased. Oh God! what *could* I do? I foamed — I raved — I swore! I swung the chair upon which I had been sitting, and grated it upon the boards, but the noise arose over all and continually increased. It grew louder — louder — *louder!* And still the men chatted pleasantly, and smiled. Was it possible they heard not? Almighty God! — no, no! They heard! — they suspected! — they *knew!* — they were making a mockery of my horror! — this I thought, and this I think. But anything was better than this agony! Anything was more tolerable than this derision! I could bear those hypocritical smiles no longer! I felt that I must scream or die! and now — again! — hark! louder! louder! louder! *louder!*

'Villains!' I shrieked, 'dissemble no more! I admit the deed!— tear up the planks! here, here! — it is the beating of his hideous heart!'

Earth to Earth

ROBERT GRAVES

Born 1895. British poet and novelist. He was Professor of Poetry at Oxford 1961-6, and is best known for a series of historical novels about the Roman emperor, Claudius.

Elsie and Roland Hedges — she a book illustrator, he an architect with suspect lungs — had been warned against Dr Eugen Steinpilz. 'He'll bring you no luck,' I told them. 'My little finger says so decisively.'

'You too?' asked Elsie indignantly. (This was at Brixham, South Devon, in March 1940.) 'I suppose you think that because of his foreign accent and his beard he must be a spy?'

'No,' I said coldly, 'that point hadn't occurred to me. But I won't contradict you.' I was annoyed.

The very next day Elsie deliberately picked a friendship — I don't like the phrase, but that's what she did — with the Doctor, an Alsatian with an American passport, who described himself as a *Naturphilosoph;* and both she and Roland were soon immersed in Steinpilzeri up to the nostrils. It began when he invited them to lunch and gave them cold meat and two rival sets of vegetable dishes — potatoes (baked), carrots (creamed), bought from the local fruiterer; and potatoes (baked) and carrots (creamed), grown on compost in his own garden.

The superiority of the latter over the former in appearance, size, and especially flavour came as an eye-opener to Elsie and Roland; and so Dr Steinpilz soon converted the childless and devoted couple to the Steinpilz method of composting. It did not, as a matter of fact, vary greatly from the methods you read about in the *Gardening Notes* of your favourite national newspaper, except that it was far more violent. Dr Steinpilz had invented a formula for producing extremely fierce bacteria, capable (Roland

7

claimed) of breaking down an old boot or the family Bible or a torn woollen vest into beautiful black humus almost as you watched.

The formula could not be bought, however, and might be communicated under oath of secrecy only to members of the Eugen Steinpilz Fellowship — which I refused to join. I won't pretend therefore to know the formula myself, but one night I overheard Elsie and Roland arguing as to whether the planetary influences were favourable; and they also mentioned a ram's horn in which, it seems, a complicated mixture of triturated animal and vegetable products — technically called 'the Mother' — was to be cooked up. I gather also that a bull's foot and a goat's pancreas were part of the works, because Mr Pook, the butcher, afterwards told me that he had been puzzled by Roland's request for these unusual cuts. Milkwort and pennyroyal and bee-orchid and vetch certainly figured among 'the Mother's' herbal ingredients; I recognized these one day in a gardening basket Elsie had left in the post office.

The Hedges soon had their first compost heap cooking away in the garden, which was about the size of a tennis court and consisted mostly of well-kept lawn. Dr Steinpilz, who supervised, now began to haunt the cottage like the smell of drains; I had to give up calling on them. Then, after the Fall of France, Brixham became a war zone whence everyone but we British and our Free French or Free Belgian allies was excluded. Consequently Dr Steinpilz had to leave, which he did with very bad grace, and was killed in a Liverpool air raid the day before he should have sailed back to New York.

I think Elsie must have been in love with the Doctor, and certainly Roland had a hero worship for him. They treasured a signed collection of all his esoteric books, each titled after a different semi-precious stone; and used to read them out aloud to each other at meals, in turns. And to show that this was a practical philosophy, not just a random assembly of beautiful thoughts about Nature, they began composting in a deeper and even more religious way than before. The lawn had come up, of course; but they used the sods to sandwich layers of kitchen waste, which they mixed with the scrapings of an abandoned pigsty, two barrowfuls of sodden poplar leaves from the recreation ground, and a sack of rotten turnips. Once I caught the fanatic gleam in Elsie's eye as she turned the hungry bacteria loose on the heap, and could not repress a premonitory shudder.

So far, not too bad, perhaps. But when serious bombing started and food became so scarce that housewives were fined for not making over their swill to the national pigs, Elsie and Roland grew worried. Having already abandoned their ordinary sanitary system and built an earth-closet in the garden, they now tried to convince neighbours of their duty to do the same, even at the risk of catching cold and getting spiders down the neck. Elsie also sent Roland after the slow-moving Red Devon cows as they lurched home along the lane at dusk, to rescue the precious droppings with a kitchen shovel; while she visited the local ash dump with a packing case mounted on wheels, and collected whatever she found there of an organic nature — dead cats, old rags, withered flowers, cabbage stalks, and such household waste as even a national wartime pig would have coughed at. She also saved every drop of their bath water for sprinkling the heaps; because it contained, she said, valuable animal salts.

The test of a good compost heap, as every illuminate knows, is whether a certain revolting-looking, if beneficial, fungus sprouts from it. Elsie's heaps were grey with this crop, and so hot inside that they could be used for haybox cookery; which must have saved her a deal of fuel. I called them 'Elsie's heaps', because she now considered herself Dr Steinpilz's earthly delegate; and loyal Roland did not dispute this claim.

A critical stage in the story came during the Blitz. It will be remembered that trainloads of Londoners, who had been evacuated to South Devon when War broke out, thereafter de-evacuated and re-evacuated and re-de-evacuated themselves, from time to time, in a most disorganized fashion. Elsie and

Roland, as it happened, escaped having evacuees billeted on them, because they had no spare bedroom; but one night an old naval pensioner came knocking at their door and demanded lodging for the night. Having been burned out of Plymouth, where everything was chaos, he had found himself walking away and blundering along in a daze until he fetched up here, hungry and dead-beat. They gave him a meal and bedded him down on the sofa; but when Elsie came down in the morning to fork over the heaps, she found him dead of heart failure.

Roland broke a long silence by coming, in some embarrassment, to ask my advice. Elsie, he said, had decided that it would be wrong to trouble the police about the case; because the police were so busy these days, and the poor old fellow had claimed to possess neither kith nor kin. So they'd read the burial service over him and, after removing his belt buckle, trouser buttons, metal spectacle case, and a bunch of keys, which were irreducible, had laid him reverently in the new compost heap. Its other contents, Roland added, were a cartload of waste from the cider factory and salvaged cow dung.

'If you mean, "Will I report you to Civil Authorities?" the answer is no,' I assured him. 'I wasn't looking at the relevant hour, and, after all, what you tell me is only hearsay.'

The War went on. Not only did the Hedges convert the whole garden into serried rows of Eugen Steinpilz memorial heaps, leaving no room for planting the potatoes or carrots to which they had been prospectively devoted, but they regularly scavenged offal from the fish market. Every Spring, Elsie used to pick big bunches of primroses and put them straight on the compost, without even a last wistful sniff; virgin primroses were supposed to be particularly relished by the fierce bacteria.

Here the story becomes a little painful for readers of a delicate disposition, but I will soften it as much as possible. One morning a policeman called on the Hedges with a summons, and I happened to see Roland peep anxiously out of the bedroom window, but quickly pull his head in again.

The policeman rang and knocked and waited, then tried the back door; and presently went away. The summons was for a blackout offence, but apparently the Hedges did not know this.

Next morning the policeman called again, and when nobody answered, forced the lock of the back door. They were found dead in bed together, having taken an overdose of sleeping tablets. A note on the coverlet ran simply:

Please lay our bodies on the heap nearest the pigsty. Flowers by request. Strew some on the bodies, mixed with a little kitchen waste, and then fork the earth lightly over.

George Irks, the new tenant, proposed to grow potatoes and dig for victory. He hired a cart and began throwing the compost into the River Dart, 'not liking the look of them toadstools'. The five beautifully clean human skeletons which George unearthed in the process were still awaiting identification when the War ended.

The Truth about Pyecraft

H. G. WELLS

*1866-1946. British. A novelist and sociologist with ideals
far in advance of his time. He was the first exponent of
science fiction stories and a novelist of world-wide fame*

He sits not a dozen yards away. If I glance over my shoulder I can
see him. And if I catch his eye — and usually I catch his eye — it
meets me with an expression ——

It is mainly an imploring look — and yet with suspicion in it.

Confound his suspicion! If I wanted to tell on him I should have
told long ago. I don't tell and I don't tell, and he ought to feel at
his ease. As if anything so gross and fat as he could feel at ease!
Who would believe me if I did tell?

Poor old Pyecraft! Great, uneasy jelly of substance! The fattest
clubman in London.

He sits at one of the little club tables in the huge bay by the fire,
stuffing. What is he stuffing? I glance judiciously and catch him
biting at the round of hot buttered teacake, with his eyes on me.
Confound him! — with his eyes on me!

That settles it, Pyecraft! Since you *will* be abject, since you *will*
behave as though I was not a man of honour, here, right under
your embedded eyes, I write the thing down — the plain truth
about Pyecraft. The man I helped, the man I shielded, and who
has requited me by making my club unendurable, with his liquid
appeal, with the perpetual 'don't tell' of his looks.

And besides, why does he keep on eternally eating?

Well, here goes for the truth, the whole truth, and nothing but
the truth!

Pyecraft—— I made the acquaintance of Pyecraft in this very
smoking room. I was a young, nervous new member, and he saw
it. I was sitting all alone, wishing I knew more of the members,

and suddenly he came, a great rolling front of chins and abdomina, towards me, and grunted and sat down in a chair close by me, and wheezed for a space, and scraped for a space with a match and lit a cigar, and then addressed me. I forget what he said — something about the matches not lighting properly, and afterwards as he talked he kept stopping the waiters one by one as they went by, and telling them about the matches in that thin, fluty voice he has. But, anyhow, it was in some such way we began our talking.

He talked about various things and came round to games. And thence to my figure and complexion. 'You ought to be a good cricketer,' he said. I suppose I am slender, slender to what some people would call lean, and I suppose I am rather dark, still—— I am not ashamed of having a Hindu great-grandmother, but, for all that, I don't want casual strangers to see through me at a glance to *her*. So that I was set against Pyecraft from the beginning.

But he only talked about me in order to get to himself.

'I expect,' he said, 'you take no more exercise than I do, and probably you eat no less.' (Like all excessively obese people he fancied he ate nothing.) 'Yet' — and he smiled an oblique smile — 'we differ.'

And then he began to talk about his fatness and his fatness; all he did for his fatness and all he was going to do for his fatness; what people had advised him to do for his fatness and what he had heard of people doing for fatness similar to his. '*A priori,*' he said, 'one would think a question of nutrition could be answered by dietary and a question of assimilation by drugs.' It was stifling. It was dumpling talk. It made me feel swelled to hear him.

One stands that sort of thing once in a way at a club, but a time came when I fancied I was standing too much. He took to me altogether too conspicuously. I could never go into the smoking-room but he would come wallowing towards me, and sometimes he came and gormandised round and about me while I had my lunch. He seemed at times almost to be clinging to me. He was a

13

bore, but not so fearful a bore as to be limited to me; and from the first there was something in his manner — almost as though he knew, almost as though he penetrated to the fact that I *might* — that there was a remote, exceptional chance in me that no one else presented.

'I'd give anything to get it down,' he would say — 'anything,' and peer at me over his vast cheeks and pant.

Poor old Pyecraft! He has just gonged, no doubt to order another buttered teacake!

He came to the actual thing one day. 'Our Pharmacopoeia,' he said, 'our Western Pharmacopoeia, is anything but the last word of medical science. In the East, I've been told——'

He stopped and stared at me. It was like being at an aquarium.

I was quite suddenly angry with him. 'Look here,' I said, 'who told you about my great-grandmother's recipes?'

'Well,' he fenced.

'Every time we've met for a week,' I said — 'and we've met pretty often — you've given me a broad hint or so about that little secret of mine.'

'Well,' he said, 'now the cat's out of the bag, I'll admit, yes, it is so. I had it——'

'From Pattison?'

'Indirectly,' he said, which I believe was lying, 'yes.'

'Pattison,' I said 'took that stuff at his own risk.'

He pursed his mouth and bowed.

'My great-grandmother's recipes,' I said, 'are queer things to handle. My father was near making me promise——'

'He didn't?'

'No. But he warned me. He himself used one — once.'

'Ah! . . . But do you think——? Suppose — suppose there did happen to be one——'

'The things are curious documents,' I said. 'Even the smell of 'em. . . No!'

But after going so far Pyecraft was resolved I should go farther. I was always a little afraid if I tried his patience too much he

14

would fall on me suddenly and smother me. I own I was weak. But I was also annoyed with Pyecraft. I had got to that state of feeling for him that disposed me to say, 'Well, *take* the risk!' The little affair of Pattison to which I have alluded was a different matter altogether. What it was doesn't concern us now, but I knew, anyhow, that the particular recipe I used then was safe. The rest I didn't know so much about, and, on the whole, I was inclined to doubt their safety pretty completely.

Yet even if Pyecraft got poisoned——

I must confess the poisoning of Pyecraft struck me as an immense undertaking.

That evening I took that queer, odd-scented sandalwood box out of my safe and turned the rustling skins over. The gentleman who wrote the recipes for my great-grandmother evidently had a weakness for skins of a miscellaneous origin, and his handwriting was cramped to the last degree. Some of the things are quite unreadable to me — though my family, with its Indian Civil Service associations, has kept up a knowledge of Hindustani from generation to generation — and none are absolutely plain sailing. But I found the one that I knew was there soon enough, and sat on the floor by my safe for some time looking at it.

'Look here,' said I to Pyecraft next day, and snatched the slip away from his eager grasp.

'So far as I can make it out, this is a recipe for Loss of Weight. ('Ah!' said Pyecraft.) I'm not absolutely sure, but I think it's that. And if you take my advice you'll leave it alone. Because, you know — I blacken my blood in your interest, Pyecraft — my ancestors on that side were, so far as I can gather, a jolly queer lot. See?'

'Let me try it,' said Pyecraft.

I leant back in my chair. My imagination made one mighty effort and fell flat within me. 'What in Heaven's name, Pyecraft,' I asked, 'do you think you'll look like when you get thin?'

He was impervious to reason. I made him promise never to say a word to me about his disgusting fatness again whatever happened — never, and then I handed him that little piece of skin.

15

'It's nasty stuff,' I said.

'No matter,' he said, and took it.

He goggled at it. 'But — but —' he said.

He had just discovered that it wasn't English.

'To the best of my ability,' I said, 'I will do you a translation.'

I did my best. After that we didn't speak for a fortnight. Whenever he approached me I frowned and motioned him away, and he respected our compact, but at the end of the fortnight he was as fat as ever. And then he got a word in.

'I must speak,' he said. 'It isn't fair. There's something wrong. It's done me no good. You're not doing your great-grandmother justice.'

'Where's the recipe?'

He produced it gingerly from his pocket-book.

I ran my eye over the items. 'Was the egg addled?' I asked.

'No. Ought it to have been?'

'That,' I said, 'goes without saying in all my poor dear great-grandmother's recipes. When condition or quality is not specified you must get the worst. She was drastic or nothing. . . . And there's one or two possible alternatives to some of these other things. You got *fresh* rattlesnake venom?'

'I got rattlesnake from Jamrach's. It cost — it cost——'

'That's your affair, anyhow. This last item——'

'I know a man who——'

'Yes. H'm. Well, I'll write the alternatives down. So far as I know the language, the spelling of this recipe is particularly atrocious. By-the-bye, dog here probably means pariah dog.'

For a month after that I saw Pyecraft constantly at the club and as fat and anxious as ever. He kept our treaty, but at times he broke the spirit of it by shaking his head despondently. Then one day in the cloakroom he said, 'Your great-grandmother——'

'Not a word against her,' I said: and he held his peace.

I could have fancied he had desisted, and I saw him one day talking to three new members about his fatness as though he was in search of other recipes. And then, quite unexpectedly his telegram came.

'Mr. Formalyn!' bawled a page-boy under my nose and I took the telegram and opened it at once.

'For Heaven's sake come. — Pyecraft.'

'H'm,' said I, and to tell the truth I was so pleased at the rehabilitation of my great-grandmother's reputation this evidently promised that I made a most excellent lunch.

I got Pyecraft's address from the hall porter. Pyecraft inhabited the upper half of a house in Bloomsbury, and I went there as soon as I had done my coffee and Trappistine. I did not wait to finish my cigar.

'Mr Pyecraft?' said I, at the front door.

They believed he was ill; he hadn't been out for two days.

'He expects me,' said I, and they sent me up.

I rang the bell at the lattice-door upon the landing.

'He shouldn't have tried it, anyhow,' I said to myself. 'A man who eats like a pig ought to look like a pig.'

An obviously worthy woman, with an anxious face and a carelessly placed cap, came and surveyed me through the lattice.

I gave my name and she opened his door for me in a dubious fashion.

'Well?' said I, as we stood together inside Pyecraft's piece of the landing.

''E said you was to come in if you came,' she said, and regarded me, making no motion to show me anywhere. And then, confidentially, ''E's locked in, sir.'

'Locked in?'

'Locked himself in yesterday morning and 'asn't let anyone in since, sir. And ever and again *swearing*. Oh, my!'

I stared at the door she indicated by her glances. 'In there?' I said.

'Yes, sir,'

'What's up?'

She shook her head sadly. ''E keeps on calling for vittles, sir

17

'*Eavy* vittles 'e wants. I get 'im what I can. Pork 'e's 'ad, sooit puddin', sossiges, noo bread. Everythink like that. Left outside, if you please, and me go away. 'E's eatin' sir, somethink *awful.*'

There came a piping bawl from inside the door: 'That Formalyn?'

'That you, Pyecraft?' I shouted, and went and banged the door.

'Tell her to go away.'

I did.

Then I could hear a curious pattering upon the door, almost like someone feeling for the handle in the dark, and Pyecraft's familiar grunts.

'It's all right,' I said, 'she's gone.'

But for a long time the door didn't open.

I heard the key turn. Then Pyecraft's voice said, 'Come in.'

I turned the handle and opened the door. Naturally I expected to see Pyecraft.

Well, you know, he wasn't there!

I never had such a shock in my life. There was his sitting-room in a state of untidy disorder, plates and dishes among the books and writing things, and several chairs overturned, but Pyecraft——

'It's all right, o' man; shut the door,' he said, and then I discovered him.

There he was right up close to the cornice in the corner by the door, as though someone had glued him to the ceiling. His face was anxious and angry. He panted and gesticulated. 'Shut the door,' he said. 'If that woman gets hold of it——'

I shut the door, and went and stood away from him and stared.

'If anything gives way and you tumble down,' I said, 'you'll break your neck, Pyecraft.'

'I wish I could,' he wheezed.

'A man of your age and weight getting up to kiddish gymnastics——'

'Don't' he said, and looked agonized. 'Your damned great-grandmother——'

18

'Be careful,' I warned him.

'I'll tell you,' he said, and gesticulated.

'How the deuce,' said I, 'are you holding on up there?'

And then abruptly I realized that he was not holding on at all, that he was floating up there — just as a gas-filled bladder might have floated in the same position. He began a struggle to thrust himself away from the ceiling and to clamber down the wall to me. 'It's that prescription,' he panted, as he did so. 'Your great-gran——'

'No!' I cried.

He took hold of a framed engraving rather carelessly as he spoke and it gave way, and he flew back to the ceiling again, while the picture smashed on to the sofa. Bump he went against the ceiling, and I knew then why he was all over white on the more salient curves and angles of his person. He tried again more carefully, coming down by way of the mantel.

It was really a most extraordinary spectacle, that great, fat, apoplectic-looking man upside down and trying to get from the ceiling to the floor. 'That prescription,' he said. 'Too successful.'

'How?'

'Loss of weight — almost complete.'

And then, of course, I understood.

'By Jove, Pyecraft,' said I, 'what you wanted was a cure for fatness! But you always called it weight. You would call it weight.'

Somehow I was extremely delighted. I quite liked Pyecraft for the time. 'Let me help you!' I said, and took his hand and pulled him down. He kicked about, trying to get foothold somewhere. It was very like holding a flag on a windy day.

'That table,' he said, pointing, 'is solid mahogany and very heavy. If you can put me under that——'

I did, and there he wallowed about like a captive balloon, while I stood on his hearthrug and talked to him.

I lit a cigar. 'Tell me,' I said, 'what happened?'

'I took it,' he said.

'How did it taste?'

19

'Oh, *beastly!*'

I should fancy they all did. Whether one regards the ingredients or the probable compound or the possible results, almost all my great-grandmother's remedies appear to me at least to be extraordinarily uninviting. For my own part——

'I took a little sip first.'

'Yes?'

'And as I felt lighter and better after an hour, I decided to take the draught.'

'My dear Pyecraft!'

'I held my nose,' he explained. 'And then I kept on getting lighter and lighter — and helpless, you know.'

He gave way suddenly to a burst of passion. 'What the goodness am I to *do?*' he said.

'There's one thing pretty evident,' I said, 'that you mustn't do. If you go out of doors you'll go up and up.' I waved an arm upward. 'They'd have to send Santos-Dumont after you to bring you down again.'

'I suppose it will wear off?'

I shook my head. 'I don't think you can count on that,' I said.

And then there was another burst of passion, and he kicked out at adjacent chairs and banged the floor. He behaved just as I should have expected a great, fat, self-indulgent man to behave under trying circumstances — that is to say, very badly. He spoke of me and of my great-grandmother with an utter want of discretion.

'I never asked you to take the stuff,' I said.

And generously disregarding the insults he was putting upon me, I sat down in his armchair and began to talk to him in a sober, friendly fashion.

I pointed out to him that this was a trouble he had brought upon himself, and that it had almost an air of poetical justice. He had eaten too much. This he disputed, and for a time we argued the point.

He became noisy and violent, so I desisted from this aspect of

20

his lesson. 'And then,' said I, 'you committed the sin of euphuism. You called it, not Fat, which is just and inglorious, but Weight. You——'

He interrupted to say that he recognised all that. What was he to *do?*

I suggested he should adapt himself to his new conditions. So we came to the really sensible part of the business. I suggested that it would not be difficult for him to learn to walk about on the ceiling with his hands——

'I can't sleep,' he said.

But that was no great difficulty. It was quite possible, I pointed out, to make a shake-up under a wire mattress, fasten the under things on with tapes, and have a blanket, sheet, and coverlid to button at the side. He would have to confide in his housekeeper, I said; and after some squabbling he agreed to that. (Afterwards it was quite delightful to see the beautifully matter-of-fact way with which the good lady took all these amazing inversions.) He could have a library ladder in his room, and all his meals could be laid on the top of his bookcase. We also hit on an ingenious device by which he could get to the floor whenever he wanted, which was simply to put the *British Encyclopaedia* (tenth edition) on the top of his open shelves. He just pulled out a couple of volumes and held on, and down he came. And we agreed there must be iron staples along the skirting, so that he could cling to those whenever he wanted to get about the room on the lower level.

As we got on with the thing I found myself almost keenly interested. It was I who called in the housekeeper and broke matters to her, and it was I chiefly who fixed up the inverted bed. In fact, I spent two whole days at his flat. I am a handy, interfering sort of man with a screwdriver, and I made all sorts of ingenious adaptations for him — ran a wire to bring his bells within reach, turned all his electric lights up instead of down, and so on. The whole affair was extremely curious and interesting to me, and it was delightful to think of Pyecraft like some great, fat blow-fly, crawling about on his ceiling and clambering round the

21

lintel of his doors from one room to another, and never, never, never coming to the club any more. . .

Then, you know, my fatal ingenuity got the better of me. I was sitting by his fire drinking his whisky, and he was up in his favourite corner by the cornice, tacking a Turkey carpet to the ceiling, when the idea struck me. 'By Jove, Pyecraft!' I said, 'all this is totally unncessary.'

And before I could calculate the complete consequences of my notion I blurted it out. 'Lead underclothing,' said I, and the mischief was done.

Pyecraft received the thing almost in tears. 'To be right ways up again——' he said.

I gave him the whole secret before I saw where it would take me. 'Buy sheet lead,' I said, 'stamp it into discs. Sew 'em all over your underclothes until you have enough. Have lead-soled boots, carry a bag of solid lead, and the thing is done! Instead of being a prisoner here you may go abroad again, Pyecraft! you may travel——'

A still happier idea came to me. 'You need never fear a shipwreck. All you need do is just slip off some or all of your clothes, take the necessary amount of luggage in your hand, and float up in the air——'

In his emotion, he dropped the tack-hammer within an ace of my head. 'By Jove!' he said, 'I shall be able to come back to the club again.'

The thing pulled me up short. 'By Jove!' I said, faintly. 'Yes. Of course — you will.'

He did. He does. There he sits behind me now stuffing — as I live! — a third go of buttered teacake. And no one in the whole world knows — except his housekeeper and me — that he weighs practically nothing; that he is a mere boring mass of assimilatory matters, mere clouds in clothing, *niente, nefas,* and most inconsiderable of men. There he sits watching until I have done this writing. Then, if he can, he will waylay me. He will come billowing up to me. . .

22

He will tell me over again all about it, how it feels, how it doesn't feel, how he sometimes hopes it is passing off a little. And always somewhere in that fat, abundant discourse he will say, 'The secret's keeping, eh? If anyone knew of it — I should be so ashamed... Makes a fellow look such a fool, you know. Crawling about on a ceiling and all that...'

And now to elude Pyecraft, occupying, as he does, an admirable strategic position between me and the door.

Timber

JOHN GALSWORTHY

*1867-1933. British. A novelist and dramatist, he was
best known for his studies of Edwardian family life.
Nowadays he is most remembered for* The Forsyte Saga.

Sir Arthur Hirries, Baronet, of Hirriehugh, in a northern county,
came to the decision to sell his timber in that state of mind —
common during the War — which may be called patrio-
profiteering. Like newspaper proprietors, writers on strategy,
shipbuilders, owners of works, makers of arms and the rest of the
working classes at large, his mood was: 'Let me serve my country.
and if thereby my profits are increased, let me put up with it, and
invest in National Bonds.'

With an encumbered estate and some of the best coverts in that
northern county, it had not become practical politics to sell his
timber till the Government wanted it at all costs. To let his
shooting had been more profitable, till now, when a patriotic
action and a stroke of business had become synonymous. A man
of sixty-five, but not yet grey, with a reddish tinge in his
moustache, cheeks, lips and eyelids, slightly knock-kneed, and with
large, rather spreading feet, he moved in the best circles in a
somewhat embarrassed manner. At the enhanced price the
timber at Hirriehugh would enfranchise him for the remainder of
his days. He sold it therefore one day of April when the War news
was bad, to a Government official on the spot. He sold it at half-
past five in the afternoon, practically for cash down, and drank a
stiff whisky and soda to wash away the taste of the transaction;
for, though no sentimentalist, his great-great-grandfather had
planted most of it, and his grandfather the rest. Royalty too had
shot there in its time; and he himself (never much of a
sportsman) had missed more birds in the rides and hollows of his

fine coverts than he cared to remember. But the country was in need, and the price considerable. Bidding the Government official good-bye, he lighted a cigar, and went across the Park to take a farewell stroll among his timber.

He entered the home covert by a path leading through a group of pear trees just coming into bloom. Smoking cigars and drinking whisky in the afternoon in preference to tea, Sir Arthur Hirries had not much sense of natural beauty. But those pear trees impressed him, greenish white against blue sky and fleecy thick clouds which looked as if they had snow in them. They were deuced pretty, and promised a good year for fruit, if they escaped the late frosts, though it certainly looked like freezing tonight! He paused a moment at the wicket gate to glance back at them — like scantily-clothed maidens posing on the outskirts of his timber. Such, however, was not the vision of Sir Arthur Hirries, who was considering how he should invest the balance of the cash down after paying off his mortgages. National Bonds — the country was in need!

Passing through the gate he entered the ride of the home covert. Variety lay like colour on his woods. They stretched for miles, and his ancestors had planted almost every kind of tree — beech, oak, birch, sycamore, ash, elm, hazel, holly, pine; a lime tree and a hornbeam here and there, and further in among the winding coverts, spinneys and belts of larch. The evening air was sharp, and sleet showers came whirling from those bright clouds; he walked briskly, drawing at his richly fragrant cigar, the whisky still warm within him. He walked, thinking with a gentle melancholy slowly turning a little sulky, that he would never again be pointing out with his shooting stick to such a guest where he was to stand to get the best birds over him. The pheasants had been let down during the War, but he put up two or three old cocks who went clattering and whirring out to left and right; and rabbits crossed the rides quietly to and fro, within easy shot. He came to where Royalty had stood fifteen years ago during the last drive. He remembered Royalty saying: 'Very pretty shooting at

25

that last stand, Hirries; birds just about as high as I like them.'
The ground indeed rose rather steeply there, and the timber was
oak and ash, with a few dark pines sprinkled into the bare greyish
twiggery of the oaks, always costive in spring, and the just
greening feather of the ashes.

'They'll be cutting those pines first,' he thought — strapping
trees, straight as the lines of Euclid, and free of branches, save at
their tops. In the brisk wind those tops swayed a little and gave
forth soft complaint. 'Three times my age,' he thought; 'prime
timber.' The ride wound sharply and entered a belt of larch,
whose steep rise entirely barred off the rather sinister sunset — a
dark and wistful wood, delicate dun and grey, whose green shoots
and crimson tips would have perfumed the evening coolness, but
for the cigar smoke in his nostrils. 'They'll have this spinney for
pit props,' he thought; and, taking a cross ride through it, he
emerged in a heathery glen of birch trees. No forester, he
wondered if they would make anything of those whitened,
glistening shapes. His cigar had gone out now, and he leaned
against one of the satin-smooth stems, under the lacery of twig
and bud, sheltering the flame of a relighting match. A hare
hopped away among the bilberry shoots; a jay, painted like a fan,
squawked and flustered past him up the glen. Interested in birds,
and wanting just one more jay to complete a fine stuffed group of
them, Sir Arthur, though devoid of a gun, followed, to see where
'the beggar's' nest was. The glen dipped rapidly, and the
character of the timber changed, assuming greater girth and
solidity. There was a lot of beech here — a bit he did not know,
for though taken in by the beaters, no guns could be stationed
there because of the lack of undergrowth. The jay had vanished,
and light had begun to fail. 'I must get back,' he thought, 'or I
shall be late for dinner.' He debated for a moment whether to
retrace his steps or to cut across the beeches and regain the home
covert by a loop. The jay, reappearing to the left, decided him to
cross the beech grove. He did so, and took a narrow ride up
through a dark bit of mixed timber with heavy undergrowth. The

26

ride, after favouring the left for a little, bent away to the right; Sir Arthur followed it hurriedly, conscious that twilight was gathering fast. It must bend again to the left in a minute! It did, and then to the right, and, the undergrowth remaining thick, he could only follow on, or else retrace his steps. He followed on, beginning to get hot in spite of a sleet shower falling through the dusk. He was not framed by Nature for swift travelling — his knees turning in and his toes turning out — but he went at a good bat, uncomfortably aware that the ride was still taking him away from home, and expecting it at any minute to turn left again. It did not, and hot, out of breath, a little bewildered, he stood still in three-quarter darkness, to listen. Not a sound save that of wind in the tops of the trees, and a faint creaking of timber, where two stems had grown athwart and were touching.

The path was a regular will-o'-the-wisp. He must make a bee line of it through the undergrowth into another ride! He had never before been amongst his timber in the dusk, and he found the shapes of the confounded trees more weird, and more menacing, than he had ever dreamed of. He stumbled quickly on in and out of them among the undergrowth, without coming to a ride.

'Here I am stuck in this damned wood!' he thought. To call these formidably encircling shapes 'a wood' gave him relief. After all, it was *his* wood, and nothing very untoward could happen to a man in his own wood, however dark it might get; he could not be more than a mile and a half at the outside from his dining-room! He looked at his watch, whose hands he could just see — nearly half-past seven! The sleet had become snow, but it hardly fell on him, so thick was the timber just here. But he had no overcoat, and suddenly he felt that first sickening little drop in his chest, which presages alarm. Nobody knew he was in this damned wood! And in a quarter of an hour it would be black as your hat! He *must* get on and out! The trees amongst which he was stumbling produced quite a sick feeling now in one who hitherto had never taken trees seriously. What monstrous growths they were! The thought that seeds, tiny seeds or saplings, planted by his ancestors could attain such huge impending and imprisoning bulk — ghostly great growths mounting up to heaven and shutting off this world, exasperated and unnerved him. He began to run, caught his foot in a root and fell flat on his face. The cursed trees seemed to have a down on him! Rubbing elbows and forehead with his snow-wetted hands, he leaned against a trunk to get his breath, and summon the sense of direction to his brain. Once as a young man he had been 'bushed' at night in Vancouver Island; quite a scary business! But he had come out all right, though his camp had been the only civilized spot within a radius of twenty miles. And here he was on his own estate, within a mile or two of home, getting into a funk. It was childish! And he laughed. The wind answered, sighing and threshing in the tree tops. There must be a regular blizzard blowing now, and, to judge by the cold, from the north — but whether north-east or north-west was the question. Besides, how to keep a definite direction without a compass, in the dark? The timber, too, with its thick trunks, diverted the wind into keen, directionless draughts. He looked up, but could make nothing of the two or three stars that he could see. It was a mess! And he lighted a second cigar with some difficulty, for he had begun to shiver. The wind in this blasted wood cut through his Norfolk jacket and crawled about his body, which had become hot from exertions, and now felt clammy and half-frozen. This would mean pneumonia, if he didn't look out! And, half feeling his way from trunk to trunk, he started on again, but for all he could tell he might be going round in a circle, might even be crossing rides without realizing, and again that sickening drop occurred in his chest. He stood still and shouted. He had the feeling of shouting into walls of timber, dark and heavy, which threw the sound back at him.

'Curse you!' he thought; 'I wish I'd sold you six months ago!' The wind fleered and mowed in the tree tops; and he started off again at a run in that dark wilderness; till, hitting his head against a low branch, he fell stunned. He lay several minutes unconscious, came to himself deadly cold, and struggled up on to his feet.

'By Jove!' he thought, with a sort of stammer in his brain; 'this is a bad business! I may be out here all night!' For an unimaginative man, it was extraordinary what vivid images he had just then. He saw the face of the Government official who had bought his timber, and the slight grimace with which he had agreed to the price. He saw his butler, after the gong had gone, standing like a stuck pig by the sideboard, waiting for him to come down. What would they do when he didn't come? Would they have the *nous* to imagine that he might have lost his way in the coverts, and take lanterns and search for him? Far more likely they would think he had walked over to 'Greenlands' or 'Berrymoor', and stayed there to dinner. And, suddenly, he saw himself slowly freezing out here, in the snowy night, among this cursed timber. With a vigorous shake he butted again into the darkness among the tree trunks. He was angry now — with himself, with the night, with the trees; so angry that he actually let out with his fist at a trunk against which he had stumbled, and scored his knuckles. It was humiliating; and Sir Arthur Hirries was not accustomed to humiliation. In anybody else's wood — yes; but to be lost like this in one's own coverts! Well, if he had to walk all night, he would get out! And he plunged on doggedly in the darkness.

He was fighting with his timber now, as if the thing were alive and each tree an enemy. In the interminable stumbling exertion of that groping progress his angry mood gave place to half-comatose philosophy. Trees! His great-great-grandfather had planted them! His own was the fifth man's life, but the trees were almost as young as ever; they made nothing of a man's life! He sniggered: And a man made nothing of theirs! Did they know they were going to be cut down? All the better if they did, and were sweating in their shoes. He pinched himself — his thoughts were becoming so queer! He remembered that once, when his liver was out of order, trees had seemed like solid, tall diseases

29

— bulbous, scarred, cavernous, witch-armed, fungoid emanations of the earth. Well, so they were! And he was among them, on a snowy pitch-black night, engaged in this death-struggle! The occurrence of the word death in his thoughts brought him up all standing. Why couldn't he concentrate his mind on getting out; why was he mooning about the life and nature of trees instead of trying to remember the conformation of his coverts, so as to re-kindle in himself some sense of general direction? He struck a number of matches to get a sight of his watch again. Great heaven! He had been walking nearly two hours since he last looked at it; and in what direction? They said a man in fog went round and round because of some kink in his brain! He began now to feel the trees, searching for a hollow trunk. A hollow would be some protection from the cold — his first conscious confession of exhaustion. He was not in training, and he was sixty-five. The thought: 'I can't keep this up much longer,' caused a second explosion of sullen anger. Damnation! Here he was — for all he could tell — standing where he had sat perhaps a dozen times on his spread shooting stick; watching sunlight on bare twigs, or the nose of his spaniel twitching beside him, listening to the tap of the beaters' sticks, and the shrill, drawn-out: 'Marrk! Cock over!' Would they let the dogs out, to pick up his tracks? No! ten to one they would assume he was staying the night at the Summertons', or at Lady Mary's, as he had done before now, after dining there. And suddenly his strained heart leaped. He had struck a ride again! His mind slipped back into place like an elastic let go, relaxed, quivering gratefully. He had only to follow this ride, and somewhere, somehow, he would come out. And be hanged if he would let them know what a fool he had made of himself! Right or left — which way? He turned so that the flying snow came on his back, hurrying forward between the denser darkness on either hand, where the timber stood in walls, moving his arms across and across his body, as if dragging a concertina to full stretch, to make sure that he was keeping in the path. He went what seemed an interminable way like this, till he was brought up all standing by trees, and could find no outlet, no continuation. Turning in his tracks, with the snow in his face now, he retraced his steps till once more he was brought up short by trees. He stood panting. It was ghastly — ghastly! And in a panic he dived this way and that to find the bend, the turning, the way on. The sleet stung his eyes, the wind fleered and whistled, the boughs sloughed and moaned. He struck matches, trying to shade them with his cold, wet hands, but one by one they went out, and still he found no turning. The ride must have a blind alley at either end, the turning be down the side somewhere! Hope revived in him. Never say die! He began a second retracing of his steps, feeling the trunks along one side, to find a gap. His breath came with difficulty. What would old Brodley say if he could see him, soaked, frozen, tired to death, stumbling along in the darkness among this cursed timber — old Brodley who had told him his heart was in poor case! . . . A gap? Ah! No trunks — a ride at last! He turned, felt a sharp pain in his knee and pitched forward. He could not rise — the knee dislocated six years ago was out again. Sir Arthur Hirries clenched his teeth. Nothing more could happen to him! But after a minute — blank and bitter — he began to crawl along the new ride. Oddly he felt less discouraged and alarmed on hands and knee — for he could use but one. It was a relief to have his eyes fixed on the ground, not peering at the tree trunks; or perhaps there was less strain for the moment on his heart. He crawled, stopping every minute or so to renew his strength. He crawled mechanically, waiting for his heart, his knee, his lungs to stop him. The earth was snowed over, and he could feel its cold wetness as he scraped along. Good tracks to follow, if anybody struck them! But in this dark forest —! In one of his halts, drying his hands as best he could, he struck a match, and sheltering it desperately, fumbled out his watch. Past ten o'clock! He wound the watch, and put it back against his heart. If only he could wind his heart! And squatting there he counted his matches — four! 'Well,' he thought grimly, 'I won't light them to show me my blasted trees. I've got a cigar left; I'll keep them for that.' And he crawled on again. He must keep going while he could!

He crawled till his heart and lungs and knee struck work; and, leaning his back against a tree, sat huddled together, so exhausted that he felt nothing save a sort of bitter heartache. He even dropped asleep, waking with a shudder, dragged from a dream armchair at the Club into this cold, wet darkness and the blizzard moaning in the trees. He tried to crawl again, but could not, and for some minutes stayed motionless, hugging his body with his arms. 'Well,' he thought vaguely, 'I *have* done it!' His mind was in such lethargy that he could not even pity himself. His matches: could he make a fire? But he was no woodsman, and, though he groped around, could find no fuel that was not soaking wet. He scraped a hole and with what papers he had in his pockets tried to kindle the wet wood: No good! He had only two matches left now, and he remembered his cigar. He took it out, bit the end off, and began with infinite precautions to prepare for lighting it. The first burned, and the cigar drew. He had one match left, in case he dozed and let the thing out. Looking up through the blackness he could see a star. He fixed his eyes on it, and leaning against the trunk, drew the smoke down into his lungs. With his arms crossed tightly on his breast he smoked very slowly. When it was finished — what? Cold, and the wind in the trees until the morning! Half-way through the cigar, he dozed off, slept a long time, and woke up so cold that he could barely summon vitality enough to strike his last match. By some miracle it burned, and he got his cigar to draw again. This time he smoked it nearly to its end, without mentality, almost without feeling, except his physical sense of bitter cold. Once with a sudden clearing of the brain, he thought faintly: 'Thank God, I sold the trees, and they'll all come down!' The thought drifted away in frozen incoherence, drifted out like his cigar smoke into the sleet; and with a faint grin on his lips he dozed off again . . .

An under-keeper found him at ten o'clock next morning blue from cold, under a tall elm tree, within a mile of his bed, one leg stretched out, the other hunched up towards his chest, with its foot dug into the undergrowth for warmth, his head cuddled into the collar of his coat, his arms crossed on his breast. They said he must have been dead at least five hours. Along one side snow had drifted against him; but the trunk had saved his back and other side. Above him, the spindly top boughs of that tall tree were covered with green-gold clusters of tiny crinkled elm flowers, against a deep blue sky — gay as a song of perfect praise. The wind had dropped, and after the cold of the night the birds were singing their clearest in the sunshine.

The did not cut down the elm tree under which they found his body, with the rest of the sold timber, but put a little iron fence round it and a little tablet on its trunk.

The House
With the Brick-Kiln

E. F. BENSON

1867-1940. British. Son of an Archbishop of Canterbury,
and one of three brothers, all writers. He wrote both
comic satire and stories of the supernatural.

The hamlet of Trevor Major lies very lonely and sequestered in a
hollow below the north side of the South Downs that stretch
westward from Lewes, and run parallel with the coast. It is a
hamlet of some three or four dozen inconsiderable houses and
cottages much girt about with trees, but the big Norman church
and the manor house which stands a little outside the village are
evidence of a more conspicuous past. This latter, except for a
tenancy of rather less than three weeks, now four year ago, has
stood unoccupied since the summer of 1896, and though it could
be taken at a rent almost comically small, it is highly improbable
that either of its last tenants, even if times were very bad, would
think of passing a night in it again. For myself — I was one of the
tenants — I would far prefer living in a workhouse to inhabiting
those low-pitched oak-panelled rooms, and I would sooner look
from my garret windows on to the squalor and grime of
Whitechapel than from the diamond-shaped and leaded panes of
the Manor of Trevor Major on to the boskage of its cool thickets,
and the glimmering of its clear chalk streams where the quick
trout glance among the waving water-weeds and over the chalk
and gravel of its sliding rapids.

It was the news of these trout that led Jack Singleton and
myself to take the house for the month between mid-May and
mid-June, but as I have already mentioned a short three weeks
was all the time we passed there, and we had more than a week of

34

our tenancy yet unexpired when we left the place, though on the very last afternoon we enjoyed the finest dry-fly fishing that has ever fallen to my lot. Singleton had originally seen the advertisement of the house in a Sussex paper, with the statement that there was good dry-fly fishing belonging to it, but it was with but faint hopes of the reality of the dry-fly fishing that we went down to look at the place, since we had before this so often inspected depopulated ditches which were offered to the unwary under high-sounding titles. Yet after a half-hour's stroll by the stream, we went straight back to the agent, and before nightfall had taken it for a month with option of renewal.

*   *   *

We arrived accordingly from town at about five o'clock on a cloudless afternoon in May, and through the mists of horror that now stand between me and the remembrance of what occurred later, I cannot forget the exquisite loveliness of the impression then conveyed. The garden, it is true, appeared to have been for years untended; weeds half-choked the gravel paths, and the flower-beds were a congestion of mingled wild and cultivated vegetations. It was set in a wall of mellowed brick, in which snap-dragon and stone-crop had found an anchorage to their liking, and beyond that there stood sentinel a ring of ancient pines in which the breeze made music as of a distant sea. Outside that the ground sloped slightly downwards in a bank covered with a jungle of wild-rose to the stream that ran round three sides of the garden, and then followed a meandering course through the two big fields which lay towards the village. Over all this we had fishing-rights; above, the same rights extended for another quarter of a mile to the arched bridge over which there crossed the road which led to the house. In this field above the house on the fourth side, where the ground had been embanked to carry the road, stood a brick-kiln in a ruinous state. A shallow pit, long overgrown with tall grasses and wild field-flowers, showed where the clay had been digged.

The house itself was long and narrow; entering, you passed direct into a square panelled hall, on the left of which was the dining-room which communicated with the passage leading to the kitchen and offices. On the right of the hall were two excellent sitting-rooms looking out, the one on to the gravel in front of the house, the other on to the garden. From the first of these you could see, through the gap in the pines by which the road approached the house, the brick-kiln of which I have already spoken. An oak staircase went up from the hall, and round it ran a gallery on to which the three principal bedrooms opened. These were commensurate with the dining-room and the two sitting-rooms below. From this gallery there led a long narrow passage shut off from the rest of the house by a red-baize door, which led to a couple more guest-rooms and the servants' quarters.

Jack Singleton and I share the same flat in town, and we had sent down in the morning Franklyn and his wife, two old and valued servants, to get things ready at Trevor Major, and procure help from the village to look after the house, and Mrs Franklyn, with her stout comfortable face all wreathed in smiles, opened the door to us. She had had some previous experience of the 'comfortable quarters' which go with fishing, and had come down prepared for the worst, but found it all of the best. The kitchen-boiler was not furred; hot and cold water was laid on in the most convenient fashion, and could be obtained from taps that neither stuck nor leaked. Her husband, it appeared, had gone into the village to buy a few necessaries, and she brought up tea for us, and then went upstairs to the two rooms over the dining-room and bigger sitting-room, which we had chosen for our bedrooms, to unpack. The doors of these were exactly opposite one another to right and left of the gallery, and Jack, who chose the bedroom above the sitting-room, had thus a smaller room, above the second sitting-room, unoccupied, next his and opening out from it.

We had a couple of hours' fishing before dinner, each of us

catching three or four brace of trout, and came back in the dusk to the house. Franklyn had returned from the village from his errand, reported that he had got a woman to come in to do housework in the mornings, and mentioned that our arrival had seemed to arouse a good deal of interest. The reason for this was obscure; he could only tell us that he was questioned a dozen times as to whether we really intended to live in the house, and his assurance that we did produced silence and a shaking of heads. But the countryfolk of Sussex are notable for their silence and chronic attitude of disapproval, and we put this down to local idiosyncrasy.

The evening was exquisitely warm, and after dinner we pulled out a couple of basket-chairs on to the gravel by the front door, and sat for an hour or so, while the night deepened in throbs of gathering darkness. The moon was not risen and the ring of pines cut off much of the pale starlight, so that when we went in, allured by the shining of the lamp in the sitting-room, it was curiously dark for a clear night in May. And at the moment of stepping from the darkness into the cheerfulness of the lighted house, I had a sudden sensation, to which, during the next fortnight, I became almost accustomed, of there being something unseen and unheard and dreadful near me. In spite of the warmth, I felt myself shiver, and concluded instantly that I had sat out-of-doors long enough, and without mentioning it to Jack, followed him into the smaller sitting-room in which we had scarcely yet set foot. It, like the hall, was oak-panelled, and in the panels hung some half-dozen of water-colour sketches, which we examined, idly at first, and then with growing interest, for they were executed with extraordinary finish and delicacy, and each represented some aspect of the house or garden. Here you looked up the gap in the fir-trees into a crimson sunset; here the garden, trim and carefully tended, dozed beneath some languid summer noon; here an angry wreath of storm-cloud brooded over the meadow where the trout-stream ran grey and leaden below a threatening sky, while another, the most careful and arresting of all, was a study of the brick-kiln. In this, alone of them all, was there a human figure; a man, dressed in grey, peered into the open door from which issued a fierce red glow. The figure was painted with miniature-like elaboration; the face was in profile, and represented a youngish man, clean-shaven, with a long aquiline nose and singularly square chin. The sketch was long and narrow in shape, and the chimney of the kiln appeared against a dark sky. From it there issued a thin stream of grey smoke.

Jack looked at this with attention.

'What a horrible picture,' he said, 'and how beautifully painted! I feel as if it meant something, as if it was a representation of something that happened, not a mere sketch. By Jove! ——'

He broke off suddenly and went in turn to each of the other pictures.

'That's a queer thing,' he said. 'See if you notice what I mean.'

With the brick-kiln rather vividly impressed on my mind, it was not difficult to see what he had noticed. In each of the pictures appeared the brick-kiln, chimney and all, now seen faintly between trees, now in full view, and in each the chimney was smoking.

'And the odd part is that from the garden side, you can't really see the kiln at all,' observed Jack, 'it's hidden by the house, and yet the artist F. A., as I see by his signature, puts it in just the same.'

'What do you make of that?' I asked.

'Nothing. I suppose he had a fancy for brick-kilns. Let's have a game of picquet.'

*   *   *

A fortnight of our three weeks passed without incident except that again and again the curious feeling of something dreadful being close at hand was present in my mind. In a way, as I said, I got used to it, but on the other hand the feeling itself seemed to gain in poignancy. Once just at the end of the fortnight I mentioned it to Jack.

'Odd you should speak of it,' he said, 'because I've felt the same. When do you feel it? Do you feel it now, for instance?'

We were again sitting out after dinner, and as he spoke I felt it with far greater intensity than ever before. And at the same moment the house-door which had been closed, though probably not latched, swung gently open, letting out a shaft of light from the hall, and as gently swung too again, as if something had stealthily entered.

'Yes,' I said. 'I felt it then. I only feel it in the evening. It was rather bad that time.'

Jack was silent a moment.

'Funny thing the door opening and shutting like that,' he said. 'Let's go indoors.'

We got up and I remembered seeing at that moment that the windows of my bedroom were lit; Mrs Franklyn probably was making things ready for the night. Simultaneously, as we crossed the gravel, there came from just inside the house the sound of a hurried footstep on the stairs, and entering we found Mrs Franklyn in the hall, looking rather white and startled.

'Anything wrong?' I asked.

She took two or three quick breaths before she answered:

'No, sir,' she said, 'at least nothing that I can give an account of. I was tidying up in your room, and I thought you came in. But there was nobody, and it gave me a turn. I left my candle there; I must go up for it.'

I waited in the hall a moment, while she again ascended the stairs, and passed along the gallery to my room. At the door, which I could see was open, she paused, not entering.

'What is the matter?' I asked from below.

'I left the candle alight,' she said, 'and it's gone out.'

Jack laughed.

'And you left the door and window open,' said he.

'Yes, sir, but not a breath of wind is stirring,' said Mrs Franklyn, rather faintly.

This was true, and yet a few moments ago the heavy hall-door had swung open and back again. Jack ran upstairs.

'We'll brave the dark together, Mrs Franklyn,' he said.

He went into my room, and I heard the sound of a match struck. Then through the open door came the light of the rekindled candle and simultaneously I heard a bell ring in the servant's quarters. In a moment came steps, and Franklyn appeared.

'What bell was that?' I asked.

'Mr Jack's bedroom, sir,' he said.

I felt there was a marked atmosphere of nerves about for which there was really no adequate cause. All that had happened of a disturbing nature was that Mrs Franklyn had thought I had come into my bedroom, and had been startled by finding I had not. She had then left the candle in a draught, and it had been blown out. As for a bell ringing, that, even if it had happened, was a very innocuous proceeding.

'Mouse on a wire,' I said. 'Mr Jack is in my room this moment lighting Mrs Franklin's candle for her.'

Jack came down at this juncture, and we went into the sitting-room. But Franklyn apparently was not satisfied, for we heard him in the room above us, which was Jack's bedroom, moving about with his slow and rather ponderous tread. Then his steps seemed to pass into the bedroom adjoining and we heard no more.

I remember feeling hugely sleepy that night, and went to bed earlier than usual, to pass rather a broken night with stretches of dreamless sleep interspersed with startled awakenings, in which I passed very suddenly into complete consciousness. Sometimes the house was absolutely still, and the only sound to be heard was the sighing of the night breeze outside in the pines, but sometimes the place seemed full of muffled movements and once I could have sworn that the handle of my door turned. That required verification, and I lit my candle, but found that my ears must have played me false. Yet even as I stood there, I thought I heard steps just outside, and with a considerable qualm, I must confess, I opened the door and looked out. But the gallery was quite empty, and the house quite still. Then from Jack's room opposite I heard a sound that was somehow comforting, the snorts of the snorer, and I went back to bed and slept again, and when next I woke, morning was already breaking in red lines on the horizon, and the sense of trouble that had been with me ever since last evening had gone.

Heavy rain set in after lunch next day, and as I had arrears of letter-writing to do, and the water was soon both muddy and rising, I came home alone about five, leaving Jack still sanguine by the stream, and worked for a couple of hours sitting at a writing-table in the room overlooking the gravel at the front of the house, where hung the water-colours. By seven I had finished, and just as I got up to light candles, since it was already dusk, I saw, as I thought, Jack's figure emerge from the bushes that bordered the path to the stream, on to the space in front of the house. Then instantaneously and with a sudden queer sinking of the heart quite unaccountable, I saw that it was not Jack at all, but a stranger. He was only some six yards from the window, and after pausing there a moment he came close up to the window, so that his face nearly touched the glass, looking intently at me. In the light from the freshly kindled candles I could distinguish his features with great clearness, but though, as far as I knew, I had never seen him before, there was something familiar about both his face and figure. He appeared to smile at me, but the smile was one of inscrutable evil and malevolence, and immediately he walked on, straight towards the house door opposite him, and out of sight of the sitting-room window.

Now, little though I liked the look of the man, he was as I have said, familiar to my eye, and I went out into the hall, since he was clearly coming to the front-door, to open it to him and learn his business. So without waiting for him to ring, I opened it, feeling sure I should find him on the step. Instead, I looked out into the empty gravel-sweep, the heavy-falling rain, the thick dusk. And even as I looked, I felt something that I could not see push by me through the half-opened door and pass into the house. Then the stairs creaked, and a moment after a bell-rang.

Franklyn is the quickest man to answer a bell I have ever seen, and next instant he passed me going upstairs. He tapped at Jack's door, entered and then came down again.

'Mr Jack still out, sir?' he asked.

'Yes. His bell ringing again?'

'Yes, sir,' said Franklyn, quite imperturbably.

I went back into the sitting-room, and soon Franklyn brought a lamp. He put it on the table above which hung the careful and curious picture of the brick-kiln, and then with a sudden horror I saw why the stranger on the gravel outside had been so familiar to me. In all respects he resembled the figure that peered into the kiln; it was more than a resemblance, it was an identity. And what had happened to this man who had inscrutably and evilly smiled at me? And what had pushed in through the half-closed door?

At that moment I saw the face of Fear; my mouth went dry, and I heard my heart leaping and cracking in my throat. That face was only turned on me for a moment, and then away again, but I knew it to be the genuine thing; not apprehension, not foreboding, not a feeling of being startled, but Fear, cold Fear. And then though nothing had occurred to assuage the Fear, it passed, and a certain sort of reason usurped — for so I must say — its place. I had certainly seen somebody on the gravel outside the house; I had supposed he was going to the front-door. I had opened it, and found he had not come to the front door. Or — and once again the terror resurged — had the invisible peering thing been that which I had seen outside? And if so, what was it? And how came it that the face and figure of the man I had seen were the same as those which were so scrupulously painted in the picture of the brick-kiln?

I set myself to argue down the Fear for which there was no more foundation than this, this and the repetition of the ringing bell, and my belief is that I did so. I told myself, till I believed it, that a man — a human man — had been walking across the gravel outside, and that he had not come to the front-door but had gone, as he might easily have done, up the drive into the high-road. I told myself that it was mere fancy that was the cause of the belief that Something had pushed in by me, and as for the ringing of the bell, I said to myself, as was true, that this had happened before. And I must ask the reader to believe also that I argued these things away, and looked no longer on the face of Fear itself. I was not comfortable, but I fell short of being terrified.

I sat down again by the window looking on to the gravel in front of the house, and finding another letter that asked, though it did not demand, an answer, proceeded to occupy myself with it. Straight in front led the drive through the gap in the pines, and passed through the field where lay the brick-kiln. In a pause of page-turning I looked up and saw something unusual about it; at the same moment an unusual smell came to my nostril. What I saw was smoke coming out of the chimney of the kiln, what I smelt was the odour of roasting meat. The wind — such as there was — set from the kiln to the house. But as far as I knew the smell of roast meat probably came from the kitchen where dinner, so I supposed, was cooking. I had to tell myself this: I wanted reassurance, lest the face of Fear should look whitely on me again.

Then there came a crisp step on the gravel, a rattle at the front-door, and Jack came in.

'Good sport,' he said, 'you gave up too soon.'

And he went straight to the table above which hung the picture of the man at the brick-kiln, and looked at it. Then there was silence; and eventually I spoke, for I wanted to know one thing.

'Seen anybody?' I asked.

'Yes. Why do you ask?'

'Because I have also; the man in that picture.'

Jack came and sat down near me.

'It's a ghost, you know,' he said. 'He came down to the river about dusk and stood near me for an hour. At first I thought he was — was real, and I warned him that he had better stand

43

farther off if he didn't want to be hooked. And then it struck me he wasn't real, and I cast, well, right through him, and about seven he walked up towards the house.'

'Were you frightened?'

'No. It was so tremendously interesting. So you saw him here too. Whereabouts?'

'Just outside. I think he is in the house now.'

Jack looked round.

'Did you see him come in?' he asked.

'No, but I felt him. There's another queer thing too; the chimney of the brick-kiln is smoking.'

Jack looked out of the window. It was nearly dark, but the wreathing smoke could just be seen.

'So it is,' he said, 'fat, greasy smoke. I think I'll go up and see what's on. Come too?'

'I think not,' I said.

'Are you frightened? It isn't worth while. Besides, it is so tremendously interesting.'

Jack came back from his little expedition still interested. He had found nothing stirring at the kiln, but though it was then nearly dark the interior was faintly luminous, and against the black of the sky he could see a wisp of thick white smoke floating northwards. But for the rest of the evening we neither heard nor saw anything of abnormal import, and the next day ran a course of undisturbed hours. Then suddenly a hellish activity was manifested.

That night, while I was undressing for bed, I heard a bell ring furiously, and I thought I heard a shout also. I guessed where the ring came from, since Franklyn and his wife had long ago gone to bed, and went straight to Jack's room. But as I tapped at the door I heard his voice from inside calling loud to me. 'Take care,' it said, 'he's close to the door.'

A sudden qualm of blank fear took hold of me, but mastering it as best I could, I opened the door to enter, and once again something pushed softly by me, though I saw nothing.

44

Jack was standing by his bed, half-undressed. I saw him wipe his forehead with the back of his hand.

'He's been here again,' he said, 'I was standing just here, a minute ago, when I found him close by me. He came out of the inner room, I think. Did you see what he had in his hand?'

'I saw nothing.'

'It was a knife; a great long carving knife. Do you mind my sleeping on the sofa in your room tonight? I got an awful turn then. There was another thing too. All round the edge of his clothes, at his collar and at his wrists, there were little flames playing, little white licking flames.'

*   *   *

But next day, again, we neither heard nor saw anything, nor that night did the sense of that dreadful presence in the house come to us. And then came the last day. We had been out till it was dark, and as I said, had a wonderful day among the fish. On reaching home we sat together in the sitting-room, when suddenly from overhead came a tread of feet, a violent pealing of the bell, and the moment after yell after yell as of someone in mortal agony. The thought occurred to both of us that this might be Mrs Franklyn in terror of some fearful sight, and together we rushed up and sprang into Jack's bedroom.

The doorway into the room beyond was open, and just inside it we saw the man bending over some dark huddled object. Though the room was dark we could see him perfectly, for a light stale and impure seemed to come from him. He had again a long knife in his hand, and as we entered he was wiping it on the mass that lay at his feet. Then he took it up, and we saw what it was, a woman with head nearly severed. But it was not Mrs Franklyn.

And then the whole thing vanished, and we were standing looking into a dark and empty room. We went downstairs without a word, and it was not till we were both in the sitting-room below that Jack spoke.

'And he takes her to the brick-kiln,' he said rather unsteadily. 'I say, have you had enough of this house? I have. There is hell in it.'

* * *

About a week later Jack put into my hand a guide-book to Sussex open at the description of Trevor Major, and I read:

'Just outside the village stands the picturesque manor house, once the home of the artist and notorious murderer, Francis Adam. It was here he killed his wife, in a fit, it is believed, of groundless jealousy, cutting her throat and disposing of her remains by burning them in a brick-kiln. Certain charred fragments found six months afterwards led to his arrest and execution.'

* * *

So I prefer to leave the house with the brick-kiln and the pictures signed F. A. to others.

A Long Spoon

JOHN WYNDHAM

1903-1969. British. Remembered most for his science fiction stories — his 'logical fantasies'. This story is one of his lighter and more humorous comments on human nature.

'I say,' Stephen announced, with an air of satisfaction, 'do you know that if I lace up the tape this way round I can hear myself talking backwards!'

Dilys laid down her book, and regarded her husband. Before him, on the table, stood the tape-recorder, an amplifier, and small sundries. A wandering network of leads connected them to one another, to the mains, to a big loudspeaker in the corner, and to the pair of phones on his head. Lengths and snippets of tape littered half the floor.

'Another triumph of science,' she said, coolly. 'As I understood it, you were just going to do a bit of editing so that we could send a record of the party to Myra. I'm quite sure she'd prefer it the right way round.'

'Yes, but this idea just came to me —'

'And what a mess! It looks as if we'd been giving someone a ticker-tape reception. What is it all?'

Stephen glanced down at the strips and coils of tape.

'Oh, those are just the parts where everybody was talking at once, and bits of that very unfunny story Charles would keep trying to tell everyone — and a few indiscretions, and so on.'

Dilys eyed the litter, as she stood up.

'It must have been a much more indiscreet party than it seemed at the time,' she said. 'Well, you clear it up while I go and put on the kettle.'

'But you must hear this,' he protested.

She paused at the door.

47

'Give me,' she suggested, 'give me one good reason — just one — why I ought to hear you talk backwards . . .' And she departed.

Left alone, Stephen made no attempt to gather the debris; instead, he pressed the playback key and listened with interest to the curious gabbeldigook that was his backwards voice. Then he stopped the machine, took off the headphones, and switched over to the loudspeaker. He was interested to find that though the voice still had a European quality it seemed to rattle through its incomprehensible sounds at great speed. Experimentally, he halved the speed, and turned up the volume. The voice, now an octave lower, drawled out deep, ponderous, impossible-sounding syllables in a very impressive way indeed. He nodded to himself and leant his head back, listening to it rolling sonorously around the room.

Suddenly there was a rushing sound, not unlike a reduced facsimile of a locomotive blowing off steam, also a gust of warm air reminiscent of a stokehole . . .

It took Stephen by surprise so that he jumped, and almost overturned his chair. Recovering, he reached forward, hastily pressing keys and turning knobs. The voice from the loudspeaker cut off abruptly. He peered anxiously into the items of his apparatus, looking for sparks, or smoke. There was neither, but it was while he was in the act of sighing his relief over this that he became, in some way, aware that he was no longer alone in the room. He jerked his head round. His jaw dropped fully an inch, and he sat staring at the figure some four feet to his rear right.

The man stood perfectly straight, with his arms pressed closely to his sides. He was tall, quite six feet, and made to look taller still by his hat — a narrow-brimmed, entirely cylindrical object of quite remarkable height. For the rest, he wore a high starched collar with spread points, a grey silk cravat, a long, dark frock-coat with silk facings, and lavender-grey trousers, with the points of black, shiny boots jutting out beneath them. Stephen had to tilt back his head to get a foreshortened view of the face. It was good-looking, bronzed, as if by Mediterranean sun. The eyes were large and dark. A luxuriant moustache swept out to join with well-tended whiskers at the points of the jaw. The chin, and lower parts of the cheeks were closely shaved. The features themselves stirred vague memories of Assyrian sculptures.

Even in the first astonished moment it was borne in upon Stephen that, inappropriate as the ensemble might be to the circumstances, there could be no doubt of its quality, nor, in the proper time and place, of its elegance. He continued to stare.

The man's mouth moved.

'I have come,' he announced, with a pontifical air.

'Er — yes,' said Stephen. 'I — er — I see that, but, well, I don't quite . . .

'You called upon me. I have come,' the man repeated, with an air of explaining everything.

Stephen added a frown to his bewilderment.

'But I didn't say a thing,' he protested. 'I was just sitting here, and —'

'There is no need for alarm. I am sure you will not regret it,' said the man.

'I am not alarmed. I'm baffled,' said Stephen. 'I don't see —'

The pontifical quality was reduced by a touch of impatience as the man inquired:

'Did you not construct the Iron Pentacle?' — Without moving his arms, he contracted three fingers of his right hand so that the lavender-gloved forefinger remained pointing downwards. 'Did you not also utter the Word of Power?' he added.

Stephen looked where the finger pointed. He perceived that some of the discarded scraps of tape did make a crude geometrical figure on the floor, just permissibly, perhaps, a kind of pentacle form. But *iron* pentacle, the man had said . . . Oh, the iron-oxide coating, of course . . . H'm pretty near the border of permissibility, too, one would think . . .

'Word of Power,' though . . . Well, it was conceivable that a voice talking backwards might stumble upon a Word of

49

practically anything . . .

'It rather looks,' he said, 'as if there had been a slight mistake — a coincidence. . .'

'A strange coincidence,' remarked the man, sceptically.

'But isn't that really the thing about coincidences? That they are, I mean,' Stephen pointed out.

'I have never heard of it happening before — never,' said the man. 'Whenever I, or any of my friends, have been summoned in this way, it has been to do business: and business has invariably been done.'

'Business . . . ?' Stephen inquired.

'Business,' the man repeated. 'You have certain needs we can supply. You have a certain object we should like to add to our collection. All that is necessary is that we could come to terms. Then you sign the pact, with your blood, of course, and there it is.'

It was the word 'pact' that touched the spot. Stephen recalled the slight smell of hot clinkers that had pervaded the room.

'Ah, I begin to see,' he said. 'This is a visitation — a raising. You mean that you are Old —'

The man cut in, with a quick frown:

'My name is Batruel. I am one of the fully accredited representatives of my Master; his plenipotentiary, holding his authority to arrange pacts. Now, if you would be so good as to release me from this pentacle which I find an extremely tight fit, we could discuss the terms of the pact much more comfortably.'

Stephen regarded the man for some moments, and then shook his head.

'Ha-ha!' he said. 'Ha-ha! Ha-ha!'

The man's eyes widened. He looked huffed.

'I beg your pardon!'

'Look,' Stephen said. 'I apologize for the accident that brought you here. But let us have it clearly understood that you have come to the wrong place to do any business — the wrong place entirely.'

Batruel studied him thoughtfully. He lifted his head, and his nostrils twitched slightly.

50

'Very curious,' he remarked. 'I detect no odour of sanctity.'

'Oh, it isn't that,' Stephen assured him. 'It simply is that quite a number of your deals have been pretty well documented by now — and one of the really consistent things about them is that the party of the second part has never failed to regret the deal, in due course.'

'Oh, come! Think what I can offer you —'

Stephen cut him short by shaking his head again.

'Save yourself the trouble,' he advised. 'I have to deal with up-to-date high-pressure salesmen every day.'

Batruel regarded him with a saddened eye.

'I am more used to dealing with the high-pressure customer,' he admitted. 'Well, if you are quite sure that there has been no more than a genuine mistake, I suppose there is nothing to be done but for me to go back and explain. This has not, to my knowledge, ever happened before — though, of course, by the laws of chance it had to happen some time. Just my bad luck. Very well, then. Good-bye — oh, dear, what have I said? — I mean *vale,* my friend. I am ready!'

His stance was already rigid; now, as he closed his eyes, his face became wooden, too.

Nothing happened.

Batruel's jaw relaxed.

'Well, say it!' he exclaimed, testily.

'Say what?' Stephen inquired.

'The other Word of Power, of course. The Dismissal.'

'But I don't know it. I don't know anything about Words of Power,' Stephen protested.

Batruel's brows came lower, and approached one another.

'Are you telling me you cannot send me back?' he inquired.

'If it needs a Word of Power I certainly can't,' Stephen told him.

An expression of dismay came over Batruel's face.

'But this is unheard of. . . What am I to do? I *must* have either a completed pact, *or* the Word of Dismissal.'

51

'All right, you tell me the Word, and I'll say it,' Stephen offered.

'But I don't know it,' said Batruel. 'I have never heard it. Everyone who has summoned me until now has been anxious to do business and sign the pact. . .' He paused. 'It really would simplify matters very greatly if you could see your way to — No? Oh, dear, this is most awkward. I really don't see what we are going to do. . .'

There was a sound at the door followed by a couple of taps on it from Dilys's toe, to indicate that she was carrying a tray. Stephen crossed to the door and opened it a preliminary chink.

'We have a visitor,' he warned her. He did not want to see the tray dropped out of sheer surprise.

'But how — ?' she began, and then, as he held the door open more widely, she almost did drop the tray. Stephen took it from her while she stood staring, and set it down safely.

'Darling, this is Mr Batruel — my wife,' he said.

Batruel, still standing rigidly straight, now looked embarrassed as well as constrained. He turned his head in her direction, and nodded it slightly.

'Charmed, Ma'am,' he said. 'I would have you excuse my style, but my movements are unhappily constricted. If your husband would do me the courtesy of breaking this pentacle. . .'

Dilys went on staring at him, and running an appraising eye over his clothes.

'I — I'm afraid I don't understand,' she complained.

Stephen did his best to explain the situation. At the end, she said:

'Well, I really don't know. . . We shall have to see what can be done, shan't we? It's so difficult — not as if he were just an ordinary D.P., I mean.' She went on regarding Batruel thoughtfully, and then added: 'Steve, if you have made it really clear to him that we're not signing anything, don't you think you might let him out of it? He does look so uncomfortable there.'

'I thank you, Ma'am. I am indeed uncomfortable,' Batruel

said, gratefully.

Stephen considered.

'Well, since he is here anyway, and we know where we stand, perhaps it won't do any harm,' he conceded. He bent down, and brushed aside some of the tape on the floor.

Batruel stepped out of the disrupted pentacle. With his right hand he removed his hat; with his left, he gave a touch to his cravat. He turned to sweep Dilys a bow, doing it beautifully too; toe pointed, left hand on a non-existent hilt, hat held over his heart.

'Your servant, Ma'am.'

He repeated the exercise in Stephen's direction.

'Your servant, Sir.'

Stephen's response was well-intentioned, but he was aware that it showed inadequately against his visitor's style. There followed an awkward pause. Dilys broke it by saying:

'I'd better fetch another cup.'

She went out, returned, and presided.

'You — er — you've not visited England lately, Mr Batruel?' she suggested, socially.

Batruel looked mildly astonished.

'What makes you think that, Mrs Tramon?' he asked.

'Oh, I — I just thought . . .' Dilys said, vaguely.

'My wife is thinking of your clothes,' Stephen told him. 'Furthermore, if you will excuse my mentioning it, you get your periods somewhat mixed. The style of your bow, for instance, precedes that of your clothes by, well, at least two generations, I should say.'

Batruel looked a little taken aback. He glanced down at himself. 'I paid particular note to the fashion last time I was here,' he said, with disappointment. Dilys broke in.

'Don't let him upset you, Mr Batruel. They are beautiful clothes — and such quality of material.'

'But not quite in the current *ton*?' said Batruel, acutely.

'Well, not quite,' Dilys admitted. 'I expect you get a bit out of

53

touch in — where you live.'

'Perhaps we do,' Batruel confessed. 'We used to do quite a deal of business in these parts up to the seventeenth and eighteenth centuries, but during the nineteenth it fell off badly. There's always a little, of course, but it is a matter of chance who is on call for different districts, and it so happens that I myself visited here only once during the nineteenth century, and not at all during the present century, until now. So you can imagine what a pleasure it was to me to receive your husband's summons; with what high hopes of a mutually beneficial transaction I presented myself —'

'Now, now! That's enough of that . . .' Stephen broke in.

'Oh, yes, of course. My apologies. The old war-horse scenting battle, you understand.'

There was a pause. Dilys regarded the visitor pensively. To one who knew her as well as her husband did, it was clear that there was a half-hearted struggle going on, and that curiosity was being allowed to pile up the points. At last she said:

'I hope your English assignments have not always been a disappointment to you, Mr Batruel?'

'Oh, by no means, Ma'am. I have the happiest recollections of visits to your country. I remember calling upon an Adept who lived near Winchester — it would be somewhere in the middle of the sixteenth century, I think — he wanted a prosperous estate, a title, and a beautiful, well-born wife. We were able to fix him up with a very nice place not far from Dorchester — his descendants hold it to this day, I believe. Then there was another, quite a young man, early in the eighteenth century, who was set upon a nice income, and the opportunity to marry into court circles. We gave satisfaction there, and his blood now runs in some very surprising places. And just a few years later there was another young man, a rather dull fellow who simply wanted to become a famous playwright and wit. That's more difficult, but we managed it. I shouldn't be surprised to find his name remembered still. He was —'

'That's all very well,' Stephen broke in. 'Nice enough for the descendants, but what happened to the protagonists?'

Batruel lifted his shoulders slightly.

'Well, a bargain is a bargain. A contract freely entered into . . .' he said, reprovingly. 'Although I have not been here myself lately,' he went on, 'I understand from my fellow representatives that requirements, though they differ in details, are much the same in principle. Titles are still popular, particularly with the wives of clients. So, too, the entrée to society — such as it has become. So is a fine country house, and nowadays, of course, we supply it with all mod. con., also a *pied-a-terre* in Mayfair. Where we used to provide a full stable we now offer a Bent-Rollsley saloon, a private aircraft perhaps . . .' he continued with a dreamy air.

Stephen felt it time to break in.

'Bent-Rollsley, indeed! You'd better read your Consumer Research handbook more carefully next time. And now I'll be obliged if you will leave off tempting my wife. She's not the one who would have to pay for it.'

'No,' Batruel agreed. 'That's a feature of woman's life. She always has to pay something, but the more she gets the less it costs her. Now your wife would have a much easier life, no work to do, servants to —'

'Will you please stop it!' Stephen told him. 'It should be clear to you by now that your system is old-fashioned. We've got wise to it. It's lost its appeal.'

Batruel looked doubtful.

'According to our bulletins the world is still a very wicked place,' he objected.

'I dare say, but the wickeder part of it hasn't any use for your old-fashioned terms. It greatly prefers to get a lot for a little if it can't get something for nothing.'

'Scarcely ethical,' murmured Batruel. 'One should have standards.'

'That may be, but there it is. Besides, we are much more closely knit now. How do you think I'd be able to square a sudden title

55

with Debrett, or sudden affluence with the Income Tax inspectors, or even a sudden mansion with the Planning Authority. One must face facts.'

'Oh, I expect all that could be managed all right,' Batruel said.

'Well, it isn't going to be. There is only one way nowadays that a man can safely become suddenly rich. It's — by Jove. . . !' He broke off abruptly, and plunged into thought.

Batruel said to Dilys:

'It is such a pity your husband is not doing himself justice. He has great potentialities. One can see that at a glance. Now, with some capital behind him there would be such opportunities, such scope. . . And the world still has so much to offer to a rich man — and to his wife, of course — respect, authority, ocean-going yachts. . . One can't help feeling he is being wasted at present . . .'

Dilys glanced at her abstracted husband.

'You feel that about him, too? I've often thought that they don't appreciate him properly in the business. . .'

'Office politics, very likely,' said Batruel. 'Many a young man's gifts are stunted by them. But with independence and a helpful wife — if I may say so, a clever and beautiful young wife — to help him, I see no reason why he should not —'

Stephen's attention had returned.

'Straight out of the Tempter's Manual; Chapter One, I should think,' he remarked scornfully. 'Now just lay off it, will you, and try to look facts in the face. Once you have grasped them, I am prepared to consider doing business with you.'

Batruel's expression brightened a little.

'Ah,' he said, 'I thought that when you had had a little time to consider the advantages of our offer —'

Stephen interrupted.

'Look,' he said. 'The first fact you have to face is that I have no use whatever for your usual terms — so you might as well stop trying to form a pressure-group with my wife.

'The second fact is this: *you're* the one who is in a jam, not me. How do you propose ever to get back to — er — well, wherever

56

you come from, if I don't help you?'

'All I'm suggesting is that you help yourself at the same time that you help me,' Batruel pointed out.

'Got only one angle about this, haven't you? Now, listen to me. I can see three possible courses before us. One: we find someone who can give us this Word of Power for your dismissal. Do you know how we set about that? — No? Well, nor do I.

'Then, two: I could ask the Vicar round here to have a shot at exorcizing you. I expect he'd be quite glad to oblige. It might even lead to his being canonized later on for resisting temptation. . . .'

Batruel shuddered.

'Certainly not,' he objected. 'A friend of mine was once exorcized back in the fifteenth century. He found it excruciatingly painful at the time, and he hasn't fully regained confidence in himself yet.'

'Very well, then, there's still a third possibility. In consideration of a nice round sum of money, with no strings attached, I will undertake to find someone willing to make a pact with you. Then when you have it safely signed, you will be able to report back with your mission honourably completed. How does that strike you?'

'No good at all,' Batruel replied promptly. 'You are simply trying to get two concessions out of us for the price of one. Our accountants would never sanction it.'

Stephen shook his head sadly.

'It's no wonder to me that your practice is slipping. In all the thousands of years you've been in business, you don't seem to have got a step beyond the idea of a first mortgage. And you're even prepared to employ your own capital when you should be using somebody else's. That's no way to get ahead. Now, under my scheme, I get some money, you get your pact, and the only capital laid out is a few shillings from me.'

'I don't see how that can be.' Batruel said, doubtfully.

'I assure you it can. It may mean your having to stay for a few weeks, but we can put you up in the spare room. Now, do you play football?'

'Football?' Batruel repeated vaguely. 'I don't think so. How does it go?'

'Well you'll have to mug up on the principles and tactics of the game. But the important point is this: a player must kick with precision. Now, if the ball is not exactly where he calculated it will be, this precision is lost, so is the opportunity, and so, eventually, the game. Have you got that?'

'I think so.'

'Then you will appreciate that just a nudge of an inch or so to the ball at a critical moment could do a lot — there wouldn't need to be any unsporting roughstuff, or mayhem. The outcome of a game could be arranged quite unsuspiciously. All it would need would be a nicely timed nudge by one of those imps you use for the practical jobs. That shouldn't be very difficult for you to arrange.'

'No,' Batruel agreed. 'It should be quite simple. But I don't quite see —'

'Your trouble, old man, is that you are hopelessly out of touch with modern life, in spite of your bulletins,' Stephen told him. 'Dilys, where is that Pools entry-form?'

Half an hour later Batruel was showing an appreciative grasp of the possibilities.

'Yes, I see,' he said. 'With a little study of the technicalities it should not be difficult to produce a loss, or a draw, perhaps even a win, as required.'

'Exactly,' approved Stephen. 'Well, there you are. I fill in the coupon — laying out several shillings on it to make it look better. You fix the matches. And I collect handsomely — without any awkward tax questions.'

'That's all very well for you,' Batruel pointed out, 'but I don't see how it is going to get me my pact, unless you —'

'Ah, now. Here we come to the next stage,' Stephen told him. 'In return, I undertake to find you a pact-signer in, shall we say, six weeks? In exchange for my winnings. Will that do? Good.

58

Then let's have an agreement about it. Dilys, bring me a sheet of writing-paper, will you, and some blood — oh, no, stupid of me, we've got blood . . .'

*   *   *

Five weeks later Stephen slid his Bentley to a stop in front of the Northpark Hotel, and a moment later Batruel came down the steps. The idea of putting him up at home had had to be abandoned after a couple of days. His impulse to tempt was in the nature of an uncontrollable reflex, and proved to be incompatible with domestic tranquillity, so he had removed to a hotel where he found the results less inconvenient, and the opportunities more varied.

He emerged from the revolving door cutting a very different figure from that of his first appearance in Stephen's sitting room. The side-whiskers had gone, though the luxuriant moustache remained. The frock-coat had been replaced by a meticulously cut grey suit, the remarkable top-hat by a grey felt, the cravat by a tie with stripes that were discreetly not quite Guards. Indeed, he now presented the appearance of a comfortably-placed, good-looking, latter twentieth-century man of about forty.

'Hop in,' Stephen told him. 'You've got the pact-form with you?'

Batruel patted his pocket.

'I always carry it. You never know . . .' he said, as they set off.

The first time Stephen had picked up the treble-chance win there had been, in spite of his hope of remaining anonymous, considerable publicity. It is less easy than it might seem to hide a windfall of £220,000. He and Dilys had taken the precaution of going into hiding before the next win was due — this time for £210,000. There had been some hesitation when it came to paying him the third cheque — £225,000 — not exactly a quibbling, for there was nothing to quibble about; the forecasts were down in ink, but there was a thoughtfulness on the part of the promoters which caused them to send representatives to see him. One of these, an earnest young man in glasses, talked with some intensity about the laws of chance, and had then produced a figure with a staggering number of noughts which he claimed to represent the odds against anyone bringing off a treble-chance three times.

Stephen was interested. His system, he said, must be even better than he had thought to win against such an astronomical unlikelihood as that.

The young man wanted to know about his system. Stephen, however, had declined to talk about it — but he had indicated that he might not be unwilling to discuss some aspects of it with the head of Gripshaw's Pools. So here they were now, on their way to an interview with Sam Gripshaw himself.

The Pools head office stood beside one of the new outer roads, set a little back behind a smooth lawn decorated with beds of salvias. Stephen was saluted by a braided porter as he slid his car into its park. A few moments later they were being shown into a spacious private office where Sam Gripshaw was on his feet to greet them. Stephen shook hands and introduced his companion.

'This is Mr Batruel, my adviser,' he explained.

Sam Gripshaw's glance at Batruel suddenly turned into a careful, searching look. He appeared to become thoughtful for a moment. Then he turned back to Stephen.

'Well, first, I should congratulate you, young man. You're by a long way the biggest winner in the whole history of the Pools. Six hundred and fifty-five thousand pounds, they tell me — very tidy, very tidy indeed. But' — he shook his head — 'it can't go on, you know. It can't go on . . .'

'Oh, I wouldn't say that,' Stephen replied amiably, as they sat down.

Again Sam Gripshaw shook his head.

'Once is good luck; twice could be extraordinarily good luck; three times gives off a pretty funny smell; four times would rock the industry; five times would just about bust it. Nobody's going to put up even his few bob against dead certs. Stands to reason. Now you've got a system you say?'

'*We've* got a system,' Stephen corrected. 'My friend, Mr Batruel —'

'Ah, yes — Mr Batruel,' said Sam Gripshaw, looking at Batruel thoughtfully again. 'I suppose you wouldn't like to tell me a little about your system?'

'You can scarcely expect us to do *that* . . .' Stephen protested.

'No, I suppose not,' Sam Gripshaw admitted. 'All the same, you might as well. You can't go on with it —'

'Because if we were to, we'd bust your industry? Well, we don't want to do that, of course. In fact that is why we are here. Mr Batruel has a proposition to put to you.'

'Let's hear it,' said Mr Gripshaw.

Batruel rose to his feet.

'You have a very fine business here, Mr Gripshaw. It would be most unfortunate if it were to lose the confidence of the public — both for them, and for yourself. I don't need to stress that, for I perceive that you have refrained from giving any publicity to my friend, Mr Tramon's, third win. Very wise of you, Sir, if I may say so. It could initiate a subtle breath of despondency. . .

'Now, I am in the fortunate position of being able to propose a means by which the risk of such a situation occurring again can be positively eliminated. It will not cost you a penny, and yet . . .' He launched himself into his temptation with the air of an artist taking up his beloved brush. Sam Gripshaw heard him through patiently to his conclusion:

'— and, in return for this — this mere formality, I am willing to undertake that neither our friend, Mr Stephen Tramon, here, nor anyone else will receive any further assistance in er — prognostication from me. The emergency will then be over, and you will then be able to pursue your business with the confidence that I am sure it so well merits.'

He produced his form of Pact with a flourish, and laid it on the desk.

Sam Gripshaw reached for it, and glanced through it. Rather to Stephen's surprise, he nodded, almost without hesitation.

'Seems straight enough,' he said. 'I can see I'm not well placed to argue. All right. I'll sign.'

Batruel smiled happily. He stepped forward, with a small, convenient penknife in his hand.

When the signing was done Sam Gripshaw wrapped a clean handkerchief round his forearm. Batruel picked up the pact and took a step back, waving it gently to dry the signature. Then he inspected it with simple pleasure, folded it with care, and placed it in his pocket.

He beamed upon them both, In his elation, his sense of period slipped again. He made his elegant eighteenth-century bow.

'Your servant, gentlemen.'

And, abruptly, he was gone, leaving nothing but the faintest trace of sulphur on the air.

It was Sam Gripshaw who broke the following silence.

'Well, that's got rid of *him* — and he can't get back until somebody raises him,' he added, with satisfaction. He turned to contemplate Stephen. 'You've not done so badly, young man, have you? *You* pocket more than half a million for selling him *my* soul. That's what I call business ability. Wish I'd had more of it when I was younger.'

'Well, you, at any rate, don't seem to be very perturbed about it,' Stephen said, with a perceptible note of relief in his voice.

'No. Doesn't worry me,' Mr Gripshaw told him. '*He's* the one who's going to be worried. Makes you think, doesn't it? Thousands of years him and his lot have been in business — and *still* got no system into it. What you need today is organization — the whole business at your finger-tips so you know where you are, and what's what. Too old-fashioned by half, that lot. Time they got some efficiency experts on to it.'

'Well, not very subtle perhaps,' agreed Stephen. 'But then, his need *is* rather specialized, and he *has* got what he was after.'

'Huh! You wait till he's had time to look in the files — if they know what files are down there. How do you think I ever managed to raise enough capital to start this place . . . ?'

62

Skin

ROALD DAHL

Born 1916. British. A specialist in the macabre, his peculiar brand of bizarre humour and alarming stories have gained him an international success.

That year — 1946 — winter was a long time going. Although it was April, a freezing wind blew through the streets of the city, and overhead the snow clouds moved across the sky.

The old man who was called Drioli, shuffled painfully along the sidewalk of the rue de Rivoli. He was cold and miserable, huddled up like a hedgehog in a filthy black coat, only his eyes and the top of his head visible above the turn-up collar.

The door of a café opened and the faint whiff of roasting chicken brought a pain of yearning to the top of his stomach. He moved on glancing without any interest at the things in the shop windows — perfume, silk ties and shirts, diamonds, porcelain, antique furniture, finely bound books. Then a picture gallery. He had always liked picture galleries. This one had a single canvas on display in the window. He stopped to look at it. He turned to go on. He checked, looked back; and now, suddenly, there came to him a slight uneasiness, a movement of the memory, a distant recollection of something, somewhere, he had seen before. He looked again. It was a landscape, a clump of trees leaning madly over to one side as if blown by a tremendous wind, the sky swirling and twisting all around. Attached to the frame there was a little plaque, and on this it said: CHÄIM SOUTINE (1894-1943).

Drioli stared at the picture, wondering vaguely what there was about it that seemed familiar. Crazy painting, he thought. Very strange and crazy — but I like it . . . Chäim Soutine . . . Soutine . .
'By God!' he cried suddenly. 'My little Kalmuck, that's who it is! My little Kalmuck with a picture in the finest shop in Paris!

Just imagine that!'

The old man pressed his face closer to the window. He could remember the boy — yes, quite clearly he could remember him. But when? The rest of it was not so easy to recollect. It was so long ago. How long? Twenty — no, more like thirty years, wasn't it? Wait a minute. Yes — it was the year before the war, the first war, 1913. That was it. And this Soutine, this ugly little Kalmuck, a sullen brooding boy whom he had liked — almost loved — for no reason at all that he could think of except that he could paint.

And how he could paint! It was coming back more clearly now — the street, the line of refuse cans along the length of it, the rotten smell, the brown cats walking delicately over the refuse, and then the women, moist fat women sitting on the doorsteps with their feet upon the cobblestones of the street. Which street? Where was it the boy had lived?

The Cité Falguière, that was it! The old man nodded his head several times, pleased to have remembered the name. Then there was the studio with the single chair in it, and the filthy red couch that the boy had used for sleeping; the drunken parties, the cheap white wine, the furious quarrels, and always, always the bitter sullen face of the boy brooding over his work.

It was odd, Drioli thought, how easily it all came back to him now, how each single small remembered fact seemed instantly to remind him of another.

There was that nonsense with the tattoo, for instance, Now, *that* was a mad thing if ever there was one. How had it started? Ah, yes — he had got rich one day, that was it, and he had bought lots of wine. He could see himself now as he entered the studio with the parcel of bottles under his arm — the boy sitting before the easel, and his (Drioli's) own wife standing in the centre of the room, posing for her picture.

'Tonight we shall celebrate,' he said. 'We shall have a little celebration, us three.'

'What is it that we celebrate?' the boy asked, without looking up. 'Is it that you have decided to divorce your wife so she can marry me?'

'No,' Drioli said. 'We celebrate because today I have made a great sum of money with my work.'

'And I have made nothing. We can celebrate that also.'

'If you like.' Drioli was standing by the table unwrapping the parcel. He felt tired and he wanted to get at the wine. Nine clients in one day was all very nice, but it could play hell with a man's eyes. He had never done as many as nine before. Nine boozy soldiers — and the remarkable thing was that no fewer than seven of them had been able to pay in cash. This had made him extremely rich. But the work was terrible on the eyes. Drioli's eyes were half closed from fatigue, the whites streaked with little connecting lines of red; and about an inch behind each eyeball there was a small concentration of pain. But it was evening now and he was wealthy as a pig, and in the parcel there were three bottles — one for his wife, one for his friend, and one for him. He had found the corkscrew and was drawing the corks from the bottles, each making a small plop as it came out.

The boy put down his brush. 'Oh, Christ,' he said. 'How can one work with all this going on?'

The girl came across the room to look at the painting. Drioli came over also, holding a bottle in one hand, a glass in the other.

'No!' the boy shouted, blazing up suddenly. 'Please — no!' He snatched the canvas from the easel and stood it against the wall. But Drioli had seen it.

'I like it.'

'It's terrible.'

'It's marvellous. Like all the others that you do, it's marvellous. I love them all.'

'The trouble is,' the boy said, scowling, 'that in themselves they are not nourishing. I cannot eat them.'

'But still they are marvellous.' Drioli handed him a tumblerful of the pale-yellow wine. 'Drink it,' he said. 'It will make you happy.'

Never, he thought, had he known a more unhappy person, or

one with a gloomier face. He had spotted him in a café some seven months before, drinking alone, and because he had looked like a Russian or some sort of an Asiatic, Drioli had sat down at his table and talked.

'You are a Russian?'

'Yes.'

'Where from?'

'Minsk.'

Drioli had jumped up and embraced him, crying that he too had been born in that city.

'It wasn't actually Minsk,' the boy had said. 'But quite near.'

'Where?'

'Smilovichi, about twelve miles away.'

'Smilovichi!' Drioli had shouted, embracing him again. 'I walked there several times when I was a boy.' Then he had sat down again, staring affectionately at the other's face. 'You know,' he had said, 'you don't look like a western Russian. You're like a Tartar, or a Kalmuck. You look exactly like a Kalmuck.'

Now, standing in the studio, Drioli looked again at the boy as he took the glass of wine and tipped it down his throat in one swallow. Yes, he did have a face like a Kalmuck — very broad and high-cheeked, with a wide coarse nose. This broadness of the cheeks was accentuated by the ears which stood out sharply from the head. And then he had the narrow eyes, the black hair, the thick sullen mouth of a Kalmuck, but the hands — the hands were always a surprise, so small and white like a lady's, with tiny thin fingers.

'Give me some more,' the boy said. 'If we are to celebrate then let us do it properly.'

Drioli distributed the wine and sat himself on a chair. The boy sat on the old couch with Drioli's wife. The three bottles were placed on the floor between them.

'Tonight we shall drink as much as we possibly can,' Drioli said. 'I am exceptionally rich. I think perhaps I should go out now and buy some more bottles. How many shall I get?'

'Six more,' the boy said. 'Two for each.'

'Good. I shall go now and fetch them.'

'And I will help you.'

In the nearest café Drioli bought six bottles of white wine, and they carried them back to the studio. They placed them on the floor in two rows, and Drioli fetched the corkscrew and pulled the corks, all six of them; then they sat down again and continued to drink.

'It is only the very wealthy,' Drioli said, 'who can afford to celebrate in this manner.'

'That is true,' the boy said. 'Isn't that true, Josie?'

'Of course.'

'How do you feel, Josie?'

'Fine.'

'Will you leave Drioli and marry me?'

'No.'

'Beautiful wine,' Drioli said. 'It is a privilege to drink it.'

Slowly, methodically, they set about getting themselves drunk. The process was routine, but all the same there was a certain ceremony to be observed, and a gravity to be maintained, and a great number of things to be said, then said again — and the wine must be praised, and the slowness was important too, so that there would be time to savour the three delicious stages of transition, especially (for Drioli) the one when he began to float and his feet did not really belong to him. That was the best period of them all — when he could look down at his feet and they were so far away that he would wonder what crazy person they might belong to and why they were lying around on the floor like that, in the distance.

After a while, he got up to switch on the light. He was surprised to see that the feet came with him when he did this, especially because he couldn't feel them touching the ground. It gave him a pleasant sensation of walking on air. Then he began wandering around the room, peeking slyly at the canvases stacked against the walls.

67

'Listen,' he said at length. 'I have an idea.' He came across and stood before the couch, swaying gently. 'Listen, my little Kalmuck.'

'What?'

'I have a tremendous idea. Are you listening?'

'I'm listening to Josie.'

'Listen to me, *please*. You are my friend — my ugly little Kalmuck from Minsk — and to me you are such an artist that I would like to have a picture, a lovely picture —'

'Have them all. Take all you can find, but do not interrupt me when I am talking with your wife.'

'No, no. Now listen. I mean a picture that I can have with me always . . . for ever . . . wherever I go . . . whatever happens . . . but always with me . . . a picture by you.' He reached forward and shook the boy's knee. 'Now listen to me, *please*.'

'Listen to him,' the girl said.

'It is this. I want you to paint a picture on my skin, on my back. Then I want you to tattoo over what you have painted so that it will be there always.'

'You have crazy ideas.'

'I will teach you how to use the tattoo. It is easy. A child could do it.'

'I am not a child.'

'*Please* . . .'

'You are quite mad. What is it you want?' The painter looked up into the slow, dark, wine-bright eyes of the other man. 'What in heaven's name is it you want?'

'You could do it easily! You could! You could!'

'You mean with the tattoo?'

'Yes, with the tattoo! I will teach you in two minutes!'

'Impossible!'

'Are you saying I do not know what I am talking about?'

No, the boy could not possibly be saying that because if anyone knew about the tattoo it was he — Drioli. Had he not, only last month, covered a man's whole belly with the most wonderful and delicate design composed entirely of flowers? What about the client who had had so much hair upon his chest that he had done him a picture of a grizzly bear so designed that the hair on the chest became the furry coat of the bear? Could he not draw the likeness of a lady and position it with such subtlety upon a man's arm that when the muscle of the arm was flexed the lady came to life and performed some astonishing contortions?

'All I am saying,' the boy told him, 'is that you are drunk and this is a drunken idea.'

'We could have Josie for a model. A study of Josie upon my back. Am I not entitled to a picture of my wife upon my back?'

'Of Josie?'

'Yes.' Drioli knew he only had to mention his wife and the boy's thick brown lips would loosen and begin to quiver.

'No,' the girl said.

'Darling Josie, *please*. Take this bottle and finish it, then you will feel more generous. It is an enormous idea. Never in my life have I had such an idea before.'

'What idea?'

'That he should make a picture of you upon my back. Am I not entitled to that?'

'A picture of me?'

'A nude study,' the boy said. 'It is an agreeable idea.'

'Not nude,' the girl said.

'It is an enormous idea,' Drioli said.

'It's a damn crazy idea,' the girl said.

'It is in any event an idea,' the boy said. 'It is an idea that calls for a celebration.'

They emptied another bottle among them. Then the boy said, 'It is no good. I could not possibly manage the tattoo. Instead, I will paint this picture on your back and you will have it with you so long as you do not take a bath and wash it off. If you never take a bath again in your life then you will have it always, as long as you live.'

'No,' Drioli said.

69

'Yes — and on the day that you decide to take a bath I will know that you do not any longer value my picture. It will be a test of your admiration for my art.'

'I do not like the idea,' the girl said. 'His admiration for your art is so great that he would be unclean for many years. Let us have the tattoo. But not nude.'

'Then just the head,' Drioli said.

'I could not manage it.'

'It is immensely simple. I will undertake to teach you in two minutes. You will see. I shall go now and fetch the instruments. The needles and the inks. I have inks of many different colours — as many different colours as you have paints, and far more beautiful . . .'

'It is impossible.'

'I have many inks. Have I not many different colours of inks, Josie?'

'Yes.'

'You will see,' Drioli said. 'I will go now and fetch them.' He got up from his chair and walked unsteadily, but with determination, out of the room.

In half-an-hour Drioli was back. 'I have brought everything,' he cried, waving a brown suitcase. 'All the necessities of the tattooist are here in this bag.'

He placed the bag on the table, opened it, and laid out the electric needles and the small bottles of coloured inks. He plugged in the electric needle, then he took the instrument in his hand and pressed a switch. It made a buzzing sound and the quarter inch of needle that projected from the end of it began to vibrate swiftly up and down. He threw off his jacket and rolled up his left sleeve. 'Now look. Watch me and I will show you how easy it is. I will make a design on my arm, here.'

His forearm was already covered with blue markings, but he selected a small clear patch of skin upon which to demonstrate.

'First, I choose my ink — let us use ordinary blue — and I dip the point of the needle in the ink . . . so . . . and I hold the needle

70

up straight and I run it lightly over the surface of the skin . . . like this . . . and with the little motor and the electricity, the needle jumps up and down and punctures the skin and the ink goes in and there you are. See how easy it is . . . see how I draw a picture of a greyhound here upon my arm . . .'

The boy was intrigued. 'Now let *me* practise a little — on your arm.'

With the buzzing needle he began to draw blue lines upon Drioli's arm. 'It is simple,' he said. 'It is like drawing with pen and ink. There is no difference except that it is slower.'

'There is nothing to it. Are you ready? Shall we begin?'

'At once.'

'The model!' cried Drioli. 'Come on, Josie!' He was in a bustle of enthusiasm now, tottering around the room arranging everything, like a child preparing for some exciting game. 'Where will you have her? Where shall she stand?'

'Let her be standing there, by my dressing-table. Let her be brushing her hair. I will paint her with her hair down over her shoulders and her brushing it.'

'Tremendous. You are a genius.'

Reluctantly, the girl walked over and stood by the dressing-table, carrying her glass of wine with her.

Drioli pulled off his shirt and stepped out of his trousers. He retained only his underpants and his socks and shoes, and he stood there swaying gently from side to side, his small body firm, white-skinned, almost hairless. 'Now,' he said, 'I am the canvas. Where will you place your canvas?'

'As always, upon the easel.'

'Don't be crazy. I am the canvas.'

'Then place yourself upon the easel. That is where you belong.'

'How can I?'

'Are you the canvas or are you not the canvas?'

'I am the canvas. Already I begin to feel like a canvas.'

'Then place yourself upon the easel. There should be no difficulty.'

71

'Truly, it is not possible.'

'Then sit on the chair. Sit back to front, then you can lean your drunken head against the back of it. Hurry now, for I am about to commence.'

'I am ready. I am waiting.'

'First,' the boy said, 'I shall make an ordinary painting. Then, if it pleases me, I shall tattoo over it.' With a wide brush he began to paint upon the naked skin of the man's back.

'Ayee! Ayee!' Drioli screamed. 'A monstrous centipede is marching down my spine!'

'Be still now! Be still!' The boy worked rapidly, applying the paint only in a thin blue wash so that it would not afterwards interfere with the process of tattooing. His concentration, as soon as he began to paint, was so great that it appeared somehow to supersede his drunkenness. He applied the brush strokes with quick short jabs of the arm, holding the wrist stiff, and in less than half an hour it was finished.

'All right. That's all,' he said to the girl, who immediately returned to the couch, lay down, and fell asleep.

Drioli remained awake. He watched the boy take up the needle and dip it in the ink; then he felt the sharp tickling sting as it touched the skin of his back. The pain, which was unpleasant but never extreme, kept him from going to sleep. By following the track of the needle and by watching the different colours of ink that the boy was using. Drioli amused himself trying to visualize what was going on behind him. The boy worked with an astonishing intensity. He appeared to have become completely absorbed in the little machine and in the unusual effects it was able to produce.

Far into the small hours of the morning the machine buzzed and the boy worked. Drioli could remember that when the artist finally stepped back and said, 'It is finished,' there was daylight outside and the sound of people walking in the street.

'I want to see it,' Drioli said. The boy held up a mirror, at an angle, and Drioli craned his neck to look.

72

'Good God!' he cried. It was a startling sight. The whole of his back, from the top of the shoulders to the base of the spine, was a blaze of colour — gold and green and blue and black and scarlet. The tattoo was applied so heavily it looked almost like an impasto. The boy had followed as closely as possible the original brush strokes, filling them in solid, and it was marvellous the way he had made use of the spine and the protrusion of the shoulder blades so that they became part of the composition. What is more, he had somehow managed to achieve — even with this slow process — a certain spontaneity. The portrait was quite alive; it contained much of that twisted, tortured quality so characteristic of Soutine's other work. It was not a good likeness. It was a mood rather than a likeness, the model's face vague and tipsy, the background swirling around her head in a mass of dark-green curling strokes.

'It's tremendous!'

'I rather like it myself.' The boy stood back, examining it critically. 'You know,' he added, 'I think it's good enough for me to sign.' And taking up the buzzer again, he inscribed his name in red ink on the right-hand side, over the place where Drioli's kidney was.

The old man who was called Drioli was standing in a sort of trance, staring at the painting in the window of the picture-dealer's shop. It had been so long ago, all that — almost as though it had happened in another life.

And the boy? What had become of him? He could remember now that after returning from the war — the first war — he had missed him and had questioned Josie.

'Where is my little Kalmuck?'

'He is gone,' she had answered. 'I do not know where, but I heard it said that a dealer had taken him up and sent him away to Céret to make more paintings.'

'Perhaps he will return.'

'Perhaps he will. Who knows?'

That was the last time they had mentioned him. Shortly

73

afterwards they had moved to Le Havre where there were more sailors and business was better. The old man smiled as he remembered Le Havre. Those were the pleasant years, the years between the wars, with the small shop near the docks and the comfortable rooms and always enough work, with every day three, four, five sailors coming and wanting pictures on their arms. Those were truly the pleasant years.

Then had come the second war, and Josie being killed, and the Germans arriving, and that was the finish of his business. No one had wanted pictures on their arms any more after that. And by that time he was too old for any other kind of work. In desperation he had made his way back to Paris, hoping vaguely that things would be easier in the big city. But they were not.

And now, after the war was over, he possessed neither the means nor the energy to start up his small business again. It wasn't very easy for an old man to know what to do, especially when one did not like to beg. Yet how else could he keep alive?

Well, he thought, still staring at the picture. So that is my little Kalmuck. And how quickly the sight of one small object such as this can stir the memory. Up to a few moments ago he had even forgotten that he had a tattoo on his back. It had been ages since he had thought about it. He put his face closer to the window and looked into the gallery. On the walls he could see many other pictures and all seemed to be the work of the same artist. There were a great number of people strolling around. Obviously it was a special exhibition.

On a sudden impulse, Drioli turned, pushed open the door of the gallery and went in.

It was a long room with a thick wine-coloured carpet, and by God how beautiful and warm it was! There were all these people strolling about looking at the pictures, well-washed dignified people, each of whom held a catalogue in the hand. Drioli stood just inside the door, nervously glancing around, wondering whether he dared go forward and mingle with this crowd. But before he had had time to gather his courage, he heard a voice

74

beside him saying, 'What is it you want?'

The speaker wore a black morning coat. He was plump and short and had a very white face. It was a flabby face with so much flesh upon it that the cheeks hung down on either side of the mouth in two fleshy collops, spanielwise. He came up close to Drioli and said again, 'What is it you want?'

Drioli stood still.

'If you please,' the man was saying, 'take yourself out of my gallery.'

'Am I not permitted to look at the pictures?'

'I have asked you to leave.'

Drioli stood his ground. He felt suddenly, overwhelmingly outraged.

'Let us not have trouble,' the man was saying. 'Come on now, this way.' He put a fat white paw on Drioli's arm and began to push him firmly to the door.

That did it. 'Take your goddam hands off me!' Drioli shouted. His voice rang clear down the long gallery and all the heads jerked around as one — all the startled faces stared down the length of the room at the person who had made this noise. A flunkey came running over to help, and the two men tried to hustle Drioli through the door. The people stood still, watching the struggle. Their faces expressed only a mild interest, and seemed to be saying, 'It's all right. There's no danger to us. It's being taken care of.'

'I, too!' Drioli was shouting. 'I, too, have a picture by this painter! He was my friend and I have a picture which he gave me!'

'He's mad.'

'A lunatic. A raving lunatic.'

'Someone should call the police.'

With a rapid twist of the body Drioli suddenly jumped clear of the two men, and before anyone could stop him he was running down the gallery shouting, 'I'll show you! I'll show you! I'll show you!' He flung off his overcoat, then his jacket and shirt, and he turned so that his naked back was towards the people.

75

'There!' he cried, breathing quickly. 'You see? There it is!'

There was a sudden absolute silence in the room, each person arrested in what he was doing, standing motionless in a kind of shocked, uneasy bewilderment. They were staring at the tattooed picture. It was still there, the colours as bright as ever, but the old man's back was thinner now, the shoulder blades protruded more sharply, and the effect, though not great, was to give the picture a curiously wrinkled, squashed appearance.

Somebody said, 'My God, but it is!'

Then came the excitement and the noise of voices as the people surged forward to crowd around the old man.

'It is unmistakable!'

'His early manner, yes?'

'It is fantastic, fantastic!'

'And look, it is signed!'

'Bend your shoulders forward, my friend, so that the picture stretches out flat.'

'Old one, when was this done?'

'In 1913,' Drioli said, without turning around. 'In the autumn of 1913.'

'Who taught Soutine to tattoo?'

'I taught him.'

'And the woman?'

'She was my wife.'

The gallery owner was pushing through the crowd towards Drioli. He was calm now, deadly serious, making a smile with his mouth. 'Monsieur,' he said, 'I will buy it.' Drioli could see the loose fat upon the face vibrating as he moved his jaw. 'I said I will buy it, Monsieur.'

'How can you buy it?' Drioli asked softly.

'I will give two hundred thousand francs for it.' The dealer's eyes were small and dark, the wings of his broad nose-base were beginning to quiver.

'Don't do it!' someone murmured in the crowd. 'It is worth twenty times as much.'

76

Drioli opened his mouth to speak. No words came, so he shut it; then he opened it again and said slowly, 'But how can I sell it?' He lifted his hands, let them drop loosely to his sides. 'Monsieur, how can I possibly sell it?' All the sadness in the world was in his voice.

'Yes!' they were saying in the crowd. 'How can he sell it? It is part of himself!'

'Listen,' the dealer said, coming up close. 'I will help you. I will make you rich. Together we shall make some private arrangement over this picture, no?'

Drioli watched him with slow, apprehensive eyes. 'But how can you buy it, Monsieur? What will you do with it when you have bought it? Where will you keep it? Where will you keep it tonight? And where tomorrow?'

'Ah, where will I keep it? Yes, where will I keep it? Now, where will I keep it? Well, now . . .' The dealer stroked the bridge of his nose with a fat white finger. 'It would seem,' he said, 'that if I take the picture, I take you also. That is a disadvantage.' He paused and stroked his nose again. 'The picture itself is of no value until you are dead. How old are you, my friend?'

'Sixty-one.'

'But you are perhaps not very robust, no?' The dealer lowered the hand from his nose and looked Drioli up and down, slowly, like a farmer appraising an old horse.

'I do not like this,' Drioli said, edging away. 'Quite honestly, Monsieur, I do not like it.' He edged straight into the arms of a tall man who put out his hands and caught him gently by the shoulders. Drioli glanced around and apologized. The man smiled down at him, patting one of the old fellow's naked shoulders reassuringly with a hand encased in a canary-coloured glove.

'Listen, my friend,' the stranger said, still smiling. 'Do you like to swim and to bask yourself in the sun?'

Drioli looked up at him, rather startled.

'Do you like fine food and red wine from the great chateâux of

77

Bordeaux?' The man was still smiling, showing strong white teeth with a flash of gold among them. He spoke in a soft coaxing manner, one gloved hand still resting on Drioli's shoulder. 'Do you like such things?'

'Well — yes,' Drioli answered, still greatly perplexed. 'Of course.'

'And the company of beautiful women?'

'Why not?'

'And a cupboard full of suits and shirts made to your own personal measurements? It would seem that you are a little lacking for clothes.'

Drioli watched this suave man, waiting for the rest of the proposition.

'Have you ever had a shoe constructed especially for your own foot?'

'No.'

'You would like that?'

'Well . . .'

'And a man who will shave you in the mornings and trim your hair?'

Drioli simply stood and gaped.

'And a plump attractive girl to manicure the nails of your fingers?'

Someone in the crowd giggled.

'And a bell beside your bed to summon a maid to bring your breakfast in the morning? Would you like these things, my friend? Do they appeal to you?'

Drioli stood still and looked at him.

'You see, I am the owner of the Hotel Bristol in Cannes. I now invite you to come down there and live as my guest for the rest of your life in luxury and comfort.' The man paused, allowing his listener time to savour this cheerful prospect.

'Your only duty — shall I call it your pleasure — will be to spend your time on my beach in bathing trunks, walking among my guests, sunning yourself, swimming, drinking cocktails. You would like that?'

There was no answer.

'Don't you see — all the guests will thus be able to observe this fascinating picture by Soutine. You will become famous, and men will say, "Look, there is the fellow with ten million francs upon his back." You like this idea, Monsieur? It pleases you?'

Drioli looked up at the tall man in the canary gloves, still wondering whether this was some sort of a joke. 'It is a comical idea,' he said slowly. 'But do you really mean it?'

'Of course I mean it.'

'Wait,' the dealer interrupted. 'See here, old one. Here is the answer to our problem. I will buy the picture, and I will arrange with a surgeon to remove the skin from your back, and then you will be able to go off on your own and enjoy the great sum of money I shall give you for it.'

'With no skin on my back?'

'No, no, please! You misunderstand. This surgeon will put a new piece of skin in the place of the old one. It is simple.'

'Could he do that?'

'There is nothing to it.'

'Impossible!' said the man with the canary gloves. 'He's too old for such a major skin-grafting operation. It would kill him. It would kill you, my friend.'

'It would kill me?'

'Naturally. You would never survive. Only the picture would come through.'

'In the name of God!' Drioli cried. He looked around aghast at the faces of the people watching him, and in the silence that followed, another man's voice, speaking quietly from the back of the group, could be heard saying, 'Perhaps, if one were to offer this old man enough money, he might consent to kill himself on the spot. Who knows?' A few people sniggered. The dealer moved his feet uneasily on the carpet.

Then the hand in the canary glove was tapping Drioli again upon the shoulder. 'Come on,' the man was saying, smiling his

79

broad white smile. 'You and I will go and have a good dinner and we can talk about it some more while we eat. How's that? Are you hungry?'

Drioli watched him, frowning. He didn't like the man's long flexible neck, or the way he craned it forward at you when he spoke, like a snake.

'Roast duck and Chambertin,' the man was saying. He put a rich succulent accent on the words, splashing them out with his tongue. 'And perhaps a *soufflé aux marrons,* light and frothy.'

Drioli's eyes turned up towards the ceiling, his lips became loose and wet. One could see the poor old fellow beginning literally to drool at the mouth.

'How do you like your duck?' the man went on. 'Do you like it very brown and crisp outside, or shall it be . . .'

'I am coming,' Drioli said quickly. Already he had picked up his shirt and was pulling it frantically over his head. 'Wait for me, Monsieur. I am coming.' And within a minute he had disappeared out of the gallery with his new patron.

It wasn't more than a few weeks later that a picture by Soutine, of a woman's head, painted in an unusual manner, nicely framed and heavily varnished, turned up for sale in Buenos Aires. That — and the fact that there is no hotel in Cannes called Bristol — causes one to wonder a little, and to pray for the old man's health, and to hope fervently that wherever he may be at this moment, there is a plump attractive girl to manicure the nails of his fingers, and a maid to bring him his breakfast in bed in the mornings.

Running Wolf

ALGERNON BLACKWOOD

*1869-1951. British. Novelist and short story writer, he
devoted himself to occult themes. He worked for some
time in Canada, where the events in this story take place.*

The man who enjoys an adventure outside the general experience
of the race, and imparts it to others, must not be surprised if he is
taken for either a liar or a fool, as Malcolm Hyde, hotel clerk on a
holiday, discovered in due course. Nor is 'enjoy' the right word to
use in describing his emotions; the word he chose was probably
'survive'.

When he first set eyes on Medicine Lake he was struck by its
still, sparkling beauty, lying there in the vast Canadian
backwoods; next, by its supreme loneliness; and lastly — a good
deal later, this — by its combination of beauty, loneliness, and
singular atmosphere, due to the fact that it was the scene of his
adventure.

'It's fairly stiff with big fish,' said Morton of the Montreal
Sporting Club. 'Spend your holidays there — up Mattawa way,
some fifteen miles west of Stony Creek. You'll have it all to
yourself except for an old Indian who's got a shack there. Camp
on the east side — if you'll take a tip from me.' He then talked for
half an hour about the wonderful sport: yet he was not otherwise
very communicative, and did not suffer question gladly, Hyde
noticed. Nor had he stayed there very long himself. If it was such a
paradise as Morton, its discoverer and the most experienced rod
in the province claimed, why had he himself spent only three days
there?

'Ran short of grub,' was the explanation offered; but to another
friend he had mentioned briefly, 'flies,' and to a third, so Hyde
learned later, he gave excuse that his half-breed 'took sick,'

81

necessitating a quick return to civilization.

Hyde, however, cared little for the explanations; his interest in these came later. 'Stiff with fish' was the phrase he liked. He took the Canadian Pacific train to Mattawa, laid in his outfit at Stony Creek, and set off thence for the fifteen-mile canoe-trip without a care in the world.

Travelling light, the portages did not trouble him; the water was swift and easy, the rapids negotiable; everything came his way, as the saying is. Occasionally he saw big fish making for the deeper pools, and was sorely tempted to stop; but he resisted. He pushed on between the immense world of forests that stretched for hundreds of miles, known to deer, bear, moose, and wolf, but strange to any echo of human tread, a deserted and primeval wilderness. The autumn day was calm, the water sang and sparkled, the blue sky hung cloudless over all, ablaze with light. Towards evening he passed an old beaver-dam, rounded a little point, and had his first sight of Medicine Lake. He lifted his dripping paddle; the canoe shot with silent glide into calm water. He gave an exclamation of delight, for the loveliness caught his breath away.

Though primarily a sportsman, he was not insensible to beauty. The lake formed a crescent, perhaps four miles long, its width between a mile and half a mile. The slanting gold of sunset flooded it. No wind stirred its crystal surface. Here it had lain since the redskin's god first made it; here it would lie until he dried it up again. Towering spruce and hemlock trooped to its very edge, majestic cedars leaned down as if to drink, crimson sumachs shone in fiery patches, and maples gleamed orange and red beyond belief. The air was like wine, with the silence of a dream.

It was here the red men formerly 'made medicine,' with all the wild ritual and tribal ceremony of an ancient day. But it was of Morton, rather than of Indians, that Hyde thought. If this lonely, hidden paradise was really stiff with big fish, he owed a lot to Morton for the information. Peace invaded him, but the excitement of the hunter lay below.

He looked about him with quick, practised eye for a camping-place before the sun sank below the forests and the half-lights came. The Indian's shack, lying in full sunshine on the eastern shore, he found at once; but the trees lay too thick about it for comfort, nor did he wish to be so close to its inhabitant. Upon the opposite side, however, an ideal clearing offered. This lay already in shadow, the huge forest darkening it towards evening; but the open space attracted. He paddled over quickly and examined it. The ground was hard and dry, he found, and a little brook ran tinkling down one side of it into the lake. This outfall, too, would be a good fishing spot. Also it was sheltered. A few low willows marked the mouth.

An experienced camper soon makes up his mind. It was a perfect site, and some charred logs, with traces of former fires, proved that he was not the first to think so. Hyde was delighted. Then, suddenly, disappointment came to tinge his pleasure. His kit was landed, and preparations for putting up the tent were begun, when he recalled a detail that excitement had so far kept in the background of his mind — Morton's advice. But not Morton's only, for the storekeeper at Stony Creek had reinforced it. The big fellow with straggling moustache and stooping shoulders, dressed in shirt and trousers, had handed him out a final sentence with the bacon, flour, condensed milk, and sugar. He had repeated Morton's half-forgotten words:

'Put yer tent on the east shore. I should,' he had said at parting.

He remembered Morton, too, apparently. 'A shortish fellow, brown as an Indian and fairly smelling of the woods. Travelling with Jake, the half-breed.' That assuredly was Morton. 'Didn't stay long, now, did he?' he added in a reflective tone.

'Going Windy Lake way, are yer? Or Ten Mile Water, maybe?' he had first inquired of Hyde.

'Medicine Lake.'

'Is that so?' the man said, as though he doubted it for some obscure reason. He pulled at his ragged moustache a moment. 'Is that so, now?' he repeated. And the final words followed him down-stream after a considerable pause — the advice about the best shore on which to put his tent.

All this now suddenly flashed back upon Hyde's mind with a tinge of disappointment and annoyance, for when two experienced men agreed, their opinion was not to be lightly disregarded. He wished he had asked the storekeeper for more details. He looked about him, he reflected, he hesitated. His ideal camping-ground lay certainly on the forbidden shore. What in the world, he wondered, could be the objection to it?

But the light was fading; he must decide quickly one way or the other. After staring at his unpacked dunnage and the tent, already half erected, he made up his mind with a muttered expression that consigned both Morton and the storekeeper to less pleasant places. 'They must have *some* reason,' he growled to himself; 'fellows like that usually know what they're talking about. I guess I'd better shift over to the other side — for tonight, at any rate.'

He glanced across the water before actually reloading. No smoke rose from the Indian's shack. He had seen no sign of a canoe. The man, he decided, was away. Reluctantly, then, he left the good camping-ground and paddled across the lake, and half an hour later his tent was up, firewood collected, and two small trout were already caught for supper. But the bigger fish, he knew, lay waiting for him on the other side by the little outfall, and he fell asleep at length on his bed of balsam boughs, annoyed and disappointed, yet wondering how a mere sentence could have persuaded him so easily against his own better judgement. He slept like the dead; the sun was well up before he stirred.

But his morning mood was a very different one. The brilliant light, the peace, the intoxicating air, all this was too exhilarating for the mind to harbour foolish fancies, and he marvelled that he could have been so weak the night before. No hesitation lay in him anywhere. He struck camp immediately after breakfast, paddled back across the strip of shining water, and quickly settled in upon the forbidden shore, as he now called it, with a contemptuous grin. And the more he saw of the spot, the better he liked it. There was plenty of wood, running water to drink, an open space about the tent, and there were no flies. The fishing, moreover, was magnificent. Morton's description was fully justified, and 'stiff with big fish' for once was not an exaggeration.

The useless hours of the early afternoon he passed dozing in the sun, or wandering through the underbrush beyond the camp. He found no sign of anything unusual. He bathed in a cool, deep pool; he revelled in the lonely little paradise. Lonely it certainly was, but the loneliness was part of its charm; the stillness, the peace, the isolation of this beautiful backwoods lake delighted him. The silence was divine. He was entirely satisfied.

After a brew of tea, he strolled towards evening along the shore, looking for the first sign of a rising fish. A faint ripple on the water, with the lengthening shadows, made good conditions. *Plop* followed *plop,* as the big fellows rose, snatched at their food, and vanished into the depths. He hurried back. Ten minutes later he had taken his rods and was gliding cautiously in the canoe through the quiet water.

So good was the sport, indeed, and so quickly did the big trout pile up in the bottom of the canoe that, despite the growing lateness, he found it hard to tear himself away. 'One more,' he said, 'and then I really will go.' He landed that 'one more,' and was in the act of taking it off the hook, when the deep silence of the evening was curiously disturbed. He became abruptly aware that someone watched him. A pair of eyes, it seemed, were fixed upon him from some point in the surrounding shadows.

Thus, at least, he interpreted the odd disturbance in his happy mood; for thus he felt it. The feeling stole over him without the slightest warning. He was not alone. The slippery big trout dropped from his fingers. He sat motionless, and stared about him.

Nothing stirred; the ripple on the lake had died away; there was no wind; the forest lay a single purple mass of shadow; the yellow sky, fast fading, threw reflections that troubled the eye and made distances uncertain. But there was no sound, no movement; he saw no figure anywhere. Yet he knew that someone watched him, and a wave of quite unreasoning terror gripped him. The nose of the canoe was against the bank. In a moment, and instinctively, he shoved it off and paddled into deeper water. The watcher, it came to him also instinctively, was quite close to him upon that bank. But where? And who? Was it the Indian?

Here, in deeper water, and some twenty yards from the shore, he paused and strained both sight and hearing to find some possible clue. He felt half ashamed, now that the first strange feeling passed a little. But the certainty remained. Absurd as it was, he felt positive that someone watched him with concentrated and intent regard. Every fibre in his being told him so; and though he could discover no figure, no new outline on the shore, he could even have sworn in which clump of willow bushes the hidden person crouched and stared. His attention seemed drawn to that particular clump.

The water dripped slowly from his paddle, now lying across the thwarts. There was no other sound. The canvas of his tent gleamed dimly. A star or two were out. He waited. Nothing happened.

Then, as suddenly as it had come, the feeling passed, and he knew that the person who had been watching him intently had gone. It was as if a currrent had been turned off; the normal world flowed back; the landscape emptied as if someone had left a room. The disagreeable feeling left him at the same time, so that he instantly turned the canoe in to the shore again, landed, and, paddle in hand, went over to examine the clump of willows he had singled out as the place of concealment. There was no one there. of course, nor any trace of recent human occupancy. No leaves, no branches stirred, nor was a single twig displaced; his keen and practised sight detected no signs of tracks upon the ground. Yet, for all that, he felt positive that a little time ago someone had crouched among these very leaves and watched him. He remained

86

absolutely convinced of it. The watcher, whether Indian, hunter, stray lumberman, or wandering half-breed, had now withdrawn, a search was useless, and dusk was falling. He returned to his little camp, more disturbed perhaps than he cared to acknowledge. He cooked his supper, hung up his catch on a string, so that no prowling animal could get at it during the night, and prepared to make himself comfortable until bedtime. Unconsciously, he built a bigger fire than usual, and found himself peering over his pipe into the deep shadows beyond the firelight, straining his ears to catch the slightest sound. He remained generally on the alert in a way that was new to him.

A man under such conditions and in such a place need not know discomfort until the sense of loneliness strikes him as too vivid a reality. Loneliness in a backwoods camp brings charm, pleasure, and a happy sense of calm until, and unless, it comes too near. It should remain an ingredient only among other conditions; it should not be directly, vividly noticed. Once it has crept within short range, however, it may easily cross the narrow line between comfort and discomfort, and darkness is an undesirable time for the transition. A curious dread may easily follow — the dread lest the loneliness suddenly be disturbed, and the solitary human feeling himself open to attack.

For Hyde, now, this transition had been already accomplished; the too intimate sense of his loneliness had shifted abruptly into the worse condition of no longer being quite alone. It was an awkward moment, and the hotel clerk realized his position exactly. He did not quite like it. He sat there, with his back to the blazing logs, a very visible object in the light, while all about him the darkness of the forest lay like an impenetrable wall. He could not see a foot beyond the small circle of his campfire; the silence about him was like the silence of the dead. No leaf rustled, no wave lapped; he himself sat motionless as a log.

Then again he became suddenly aware that the person who watched him had returned, and that same intent and concentrated gaze as before was fixed upon him where he lay.

There was no warning; he heard no stealthy tread or snapping of dry twigs, yet the owner of those steady eyes was very close to him, probably not a dozen feet away. This sense of proximity was overwhelming.

It is unquestionable that a shiver ran down his spine. This time, moreover, he felt positive that the man crouched just beyond the firelight, the distance he himself could see being nicely calculated, and straight in front of him. For some minutes he sat without stirring a single muscle, yet with each muscle ready and alert, straining his eyes in vain to pierce the darkness, but only succeeding in dazzling his sight with the reflected light. Then, as he shifted his position slowly, cautiously, to obtain another angle of vision, his heart gave two big thumps against his ribs and the hair seemed to rise on his scalp with the sense of cold that shot horribly up his spine. In the darkness facing him he saw two small and greenish circles that were certainly a pair of eyes, yet not the eyes of Indian, hunter, or of any human being. It was a pair of animal eyes that stared so fixedly at him out of the night. And this certainly had an immediate and natural effect upon him.

For, at the menace of those eyes, the fears of millions of long dead hunters since the dawn of time woke in him. Hotel clerk though he was, heredity surged through him in an automatic wave of instinct. His hand groped for a weapon. His fingers fell on the iron head of his small camp axe, and at once he was himself again. Confidence returned; the vague, superstitious dread was gone. This was a bear or wolf that smelt his catch and came to steal it. With beings of that sort he knew instinctively how to deal, yet admitting, by this very instinct, that his original dread had been of quite another kind.

'I'll damned quick find out what it is,' he exclaimed aloud, and snatching a burning brand from the fire, he hurled it with good aim straight at the eyes of the beast before him.

The bit of pitch-pine fell in a shower of sparks that lit the dry grass this side of the animal, flared up a moment, then died quickly down again. But in that instant of bright illumination he saw clearly what his unwelcome visitor was. A big timber wolf sat on its hindquarters, staring steadily at him through the firelight. He saw its legs and shoulders, he saw its hair, he saw also the big hemlock trunks lit up behind it, and the willow scrub on each side. It formed a vivid, clear-cut picture shown in clear detail by the momentary blaze. To his amazement, however, the wolf did not turn and bolt away from the burning log, but withdrew a few yards only, and sat there again on its haunches, staring, staring as before. Heavens, how it stared! He 'shoo-ed' it, but without effect; it did not budge. He did not waste another good log on it, for his fear was dissipated now; a timber wolf was a timber wolf, and it might sit there as long as it pleased, provided it did not try to steal his catch. No alarm was in him any more. He knew that wolves were harmless in the summer and autumn, and even when 'packed' in the winter, they would attack a man only when suffering desperate hunger. So he lay and watched the beast, threw bits of stick in its direction, even talked to it, wondering only that it never moved. 'You can stay there for ever, if you like,' he remarked to it aloud, 'for you cannot get at my fish, and the rest of the grub I shall take into the tent with me!'

The creature blinked its bright green eyes, but made no move.

Why, then, if his fear was gone, did he think of certain things as he rolled himself in the Hudson Bay blankets before going to sleep? The immobility of the animal was strange, its refusal to turn and bolt was still stranger. Never before had he known a wild creature that was not afraid of fire. Why did it sit and watch him, as with purpose in its dreadful eyes? How had he felt its presence earlier and instantly? A timber wolf, especially a solitary timber wolf, was a timid thing, yet this one feared neither man nor fire. Now, as he lay there wrapped in his blankets inside the cosy tent, it sat outside beneath the stars, beside the fading embers, the wind chilly in its fur, the ground cooling beneath its planted paws, watching him, steadily watching him, perhaps until the dawn.

It was unusual, it was strange. Having neither imagination nor tradition, he called upon no store of racial visions. Matter of fact, a hotel clerk on a fishing holiday, he lay there in his blankets, merely wondering and puzzled. A timber wolf was a timber wolf and nothing more. Yet this timber wolf — the idea haunted him — was different. In a word, the deeper part of his original uneasiness remained. He tossed about, he shivered sometimes in his broken sleep; he did not go out to see, but he woke early and unrefreshed.

Again, with the sunshine and the morning wind, however, the incident of the night before was forgotten, almost unreal. His hunting zeal was uppermost. The tea and fish were delicious, his pipe had never tasted so good, the glory of this lonely lake amid primeval forests went to his head a little; he was a hunter before the Lord, and nothing else. He tried the edge of the lake, and in the excitement of playing a big fish, knew suddenly that *it,* the wolf, was there. He paused with the rod, exactly as if struck. He looked about him, he looked in a definite direction. The brilliant sunshine made every smallest detail clear and sharp — boulders of granite, burned stems, crimson sumach, pebbles along the shore in neat, separate detail — without revealing where the watcher hid. Then, his sight wandering farther inshore among the tangled undergrowth, he suddenly picked up the familiar, half-expected outline. The wolf was lying behind a granite boulder, so that only the head, the muzzle, and the eyes were visible. It merged in its background. Had he not known it was a wolf, he could never have separated it from the landscape. The eyes shone in the sunlight.

There it lay. He looked straight at it. Their eyes, in fact, actually met full and square. 'Great Scott!' he exclaimed aloud. 'Why, it's like looking at a human being!' From that moment, unwittingly, he established a singular personal relation with the beast. And what followed confirmed this undesirable impression, for the animal rose instantly and came down in leisurely fashion to the shore, where it stood looking back at him. It stood and stared into his eyes like some great wild dog, so that he was aware of a new and almost incredible sensation — that it courted recognition.

'Well, well,' he exclaimed again, relieving his feelings by addressing it aloud, 'if this doesn't beat everything I ever saw! What d'you want, anyway?'

He examined it now more carefully. He had never seen a wolf so big before; it was a tremendous beast, a nasty customer to tackle, he reflected, if it ever came to that. It stood there absolutely fearless and full of confidence. In the clear sunlight he took in every detail of it — a huge, shaggy, lean-flanked timber wolf, its wicked eyes staring straight into his own, almost with a kind of purpose in them. He saw its great jaws, its teeth, and its tongue, hung out, dropping saliva a little. And yet the idea of its savagery, its fierceness, was very little in him.

He was amazed and puzzled beyond belief. He wished the Indian would come back. He did not understand this strange behaviour in an animal. Its eyes, the odd expression in them, gave him a queer, unusual, difficult feeling. Had his nerves gone wrong, he almost wondered.

The beast stood on the shore and looked at him. He wished for the first time that he had brought a rifle. With a resounding smack he brought his paddle down flat upon the water, using all his strength, till the echoes rang as from a pistol-shot that was audible from one end of the lake to the other. The wolf never stirred. He shouted, but the beast remained unmoved. He blinked his eyes, speaking as to a dog, a domestic animal, a creature accustomed to human ways. It blinked its eyes in return.

At length, increasing his distance from the shore, he continued fishing, and the excitement of the marvellous sport held his attention — his surface attention, at any rate. At times he almost forgot the attendant beast; yet whenever he looked up, he saw it there. And worse; when he slowly paddled home again, he observed it trotting along the shore as though to keep him company. Crossing a little bay, he spurted, hoping to reach the other point before his undesired and undesirable attendant. Instantly the brute broke into that rapid, tireless lope that, except

91

on ice, can run down anything on four legs in the woods. When he reached the distant point, the wolf was waiting for him. He raised his paddle from the water, pausing a moment for reflection; for this very close attention — there were dusk and night yet to come — he certainly did not relish. His camp was near; he had to land; he felt uncomfortable even in the sunshine of broad day, when, to his keen relief, about half a mile from the tent, he saw the creature suddenly stop and sit down in the open. He waited a moment, then paddled on. It did not follow. There was no attempt to move; it merely sat and watched him. After a few hundred yards, he looked back. It was still sitting where he left it. And the absurd, yet significant, feeling came to him that the beast divined his thought, his anxiety, his dread, and was now showing him as well as it could, that it entertained no hostile feeling and did not meditate attack.

He turned the canoe towards the shore; he landed; he cooked his supper in the dusk; the animal made no sign. Not far away it certainly lay and watched, but it did not advance. And to Hyde, observant now in a new way, came one sharp, vivid reminder of the strange atmosphere into which his commonplace personality had strayed: he suddenly recalled that his relations with the beast, already established, had progressed distinctly a stage further. This startled him, yet without the accompanying alarm he must certainly have felt twenty-four hours before. He had an understanding with the wolf. He was aware of friendly thoughts towards it. He even went so far as to set out a few big fish on the spot where he had first seen it sitting the previous night. 'If he comes,' he thought, 'he is welcome to them. I've got plenty, anyway.' He thought of it now as 'he'.

Yet the wolf made no appearance until he was in the act of entering his tent a good deal later. It was close on ten o'clock, whereas nine was his hour, and late at that, for turning in. He had, therefore, unconsciously been waiting for him. Then, as he was closing the flap, he saw the eyes close to where he had placed the fish. He waited, hiding himself, and expecting to hear sounds of munching jaws; but all was silence. Only the eyes glowed steadily out of the background of pitch darkness. He closed the flap. He had not the slightest fear. In ten minutes he was sound asleep.

He could not have slept very long, for when he woke up he could see the shine of a faint red light through the canvas, and the fire had not died down completely. He rose and cautiously peeped out. The air was very cold; he saw his breath. But he also saw the wolf, for it had come in, and was sitting by the dying embers, not two yards away from where he crouched behind the flap. And this time, at these very close quarters, there was something in the attitude of the big wild thing that caught his attention with a vivid thrill of startled surprise and a sudden shock of cold that held him spellbound. He stared, unable to believe his eyes; for the wolf's attitude conveyed to him something familiar that at first he was unable to explain. Its pose reached him in the terms of another thing with which he was entirely at home. What was it? Did his senses betray him? Was he still asleep and dreaming?

Then, suddenly, with a start of uncanny recognition, he knew. Its attitude was that of a dog. Having found the clue, his mind then made an awful leap. For it was, after all, no dog its appearance aped, but something nearer to himself, and more familiar still. Good heavens! It sat there with the pose, the attitude, the gesture in repose of something almost human. And then, with a second shock of biting wonder, it came to him like a revelation. The wolf sat beside that camp-fire as a man might sit.

Before he could weigh his extraordinary discovery, before he could examine it in detail or with care, the animal, sitting in this ghastly fashion, seemed to feel his eyes fixed on it. It slowly turned and looked him in the face, and for the first time Hyde felt a full-blooded, superstitious fear flood through his entire being. He seemed transfixed with that nameless terror that is said to attack human beings who suddenly face the dead, finding themselves bereft of speech and movement. This moment of paralysis certainly occurred. Its passing, however, was as singular as its advent. For almost at once he was aware of something beyond and above this mockery of human attitude and pose, something that ran along unaccustomed nerves and reached his feeling, even perhaps his heart. The revulsion was extraordinary, its result still more extraordinary and unexpected. Yet the fact remains. He was aware of another thing that had the effect of stilling his terror as soon as it was born. He was aware of appeal, silent, half expressed, yet vastly pathetic. He saw in the savage eyes a beseeching, even a yearning, expression that changed his mood as by magic from dread to natural sympathy. The great grey brute, symbol of cruel ferocity, sat there beside his dying fire and appealed for help.

This gulf betwixt animal and human seemed in that instant bridged. It was, of course, incredible. Hyde, sleep still possibly clinging to his inner being with the shades and half shapes of dream yet about his soul, acknowledged, how he knew not, the amazing fact. He found himself nodding to the brute in half consent, and instantly, without more ado, the lean grey shape rose like a wraith and trotted off swiftly, but with stealthy tread, into the background of the night.

When Hyde woke in the morning his first impression was that he must have dreamed the entire incident. His practical nature asserted itself. There was a bite in the fresh autumn air; the bright sun allowed no half lights anywhere; he felt brisk in mind and body. Reviewing what had happened, he came to the conclusion that it was utterly vain to speculate; no possible explanation of the animal's behaviour occurred to him: he was dealing with something entirely outside his experience. His fear, however, had completely left him. The odd sense of friendliness remained. The beast had a definite purpose, and he himself was included in that purpose. His sympathy held good.

But with the sympathy there was also an intense curiosity. 'If it shows itself again,' he told himself, 'I'll go up close and find out what it wants.' The fish laid out the night before had not been touched.

It must have been a full hour after breakfast when he next saw the brute; it was standing on the edge of the clearing, looking at him in the way now become familiar. Hyde immediately picked up his axe and advanced towards it boldly, keeping his eyes fixed straight upon its own. There was nervousness in him, but kept well under; nothing betrayed it; step by step he drew nearer until some ten yards separated them. The wolf had not stirred a muscle as yet. Its jaws hung open, its eyes observed him intently; it allowed him to approach without a sign of what its mood might be. Then, with these ten yards between them, it turned abruptly and moved slowly off, looking back first over one shoulder and then over the other, exactly as a dog might do, to see if he was following.

A singular journey it was they then made together, animal and man. The trees surrounded them at once, for they left the lake behind them, entering the tangled bush beyond. The beast, Hyde noticed, obviously picked the easiest track for him to follow; for obstacles that meant nothing to the four-legged expert, yet were difficult for a man, were carefully avoided with an almost uncanny skill, while yet the general direction was accurately kept. Occasionally there were windfalls to be surmounted; but though the wolf bounded over these with ease, it was always waiting for the man on the other side after he had laboriously climbed over. Deeper and deeper into the heart of the lonely forest they penetrated in this singular fashion, cutting across the arc of the lake's crescent, it seemed to Hyde; for after two miles or so, he recognized the big rocky bluff that overhung the water at its northern end. This outstanding bluff he had seen from his camp, one side of it falling sheer into the water; it was probably the spot, he imagined, where the Indians held their medicine-making ceremonies, for it stood out in isolated fashion, and its top formed a private plateau not easy of access. And it was here, close to a big spruce at the foot of the bluff upon the forest side, that the wolf stopped suddenly and for the first time since its appearance gave audible expression of its feelings. It sat down on its haunches, lifted its muzzle with open jaws, and gave vent to a subdued and longdrawn howl that was more like the wail of a dog, than the fierce barking cry associated with a wolf.

By this time Hyde had lost not only fear, but caution too; nor, oddly enough, did this warning howl revive a sign of unwelcome emotion in him. In that curious sound he detected the same message that the eyes conveyed — appeal for help. He paused, nevertheless, a little startled, and while the wolf sat waiting for him, he looked about him quickly. There was young timber here; it had once been a small clearing, evidently. Axe and fire had done their work, but there was evidence to an experienced eye that it was Indians and not white men who had once been busy here. Some part of the medicine ritual, doubtless, took place in the little clearing, thought the man, as he advanced again towards his patient leader. The end of their queer journey, he felt, was close at hand.

He had not taken two steps before the animal got up and moved very slowly in the direction of some low bushes that formed a clump just beyond. It entered these, first looking back to make sure that its companion watched. The bushes hid it; a moment later it emerged again. Twice it performed this pantomime, each time, as it reappeared, standing still and staring at the man with as distinct an expression of appeal in the eyes as an animal may compass, probably. Its excitement, meanwhile, certainly increased, and this excitement was, with equal certainty, communicated to the man. Hyde made up his mind quickly. Gripping his axe tightly, and ready to use it at the first hint of malice, he moved slowly nearer to the bushes, wondering with something of a tremor what would happen.

If he expected to be startled, his expectation was at once fulfilled; but it was the behaviour of the beast that made him jump. It positively frisked about him like a happy dog. It frisked for joy. Its excitement was intense, yet from its open mouth no sound was audible. With a sudden leap, then, it bounded past him into the clump of bushes, against whose very edge he stood, and began scraping vigorously at the ground. Hyde stood and stared, amazement and interest now banishing all his nervousness, even when the beast, in its violent scraping, actually touched his body with its own. He had, perhaps, the feeling that he was in a dream, one of those fantastic dreams in which things may happen without involving an adequate surprise; for otherwise the manner of scraping and scratching at the ground must have seemed an impossible phenomenon. No wolf, no dog certainly, used its paws in the way those paws were working. Hyde had the odd, distressing sensation that it was hands, not paws, he watched. And yet, somehow, the natural, adequate surprise he should have felt was absent. The strange action seemed not entirely unnatural. In his heart some deep hidden spring of sympathy and pity stirred instead. He was aware of pathos.

The wolf stopped in its task and looked up into his face. Hyde acted without hesitation then. Afterwards he was wholly at a loss to explain his own conduct. It seemed he knew what to do, divined what was asked, expected of him. Between his mind and the dumb desire yearning through the savage animal there was intelligent and intelligible communication. He cut a stake and sharpened it, for the stones would blunt his axe-edge. He entered the clump of bushes to complete the digging his four-legged companion had begun. And while he worked, though he did not forget the close proximity of the wolf, he paid no attention to it; often his back was turned as he stooped over the laborious clearing away of the hard earth; no uneasiness or sense of danger was in him any more. The wolf sat outside the clump and watched the operations. Its concentrated attention, its patience, its intense eagerness, the gentleness and docility of the grey, fierce, and probably hungry brute, its obvious pleasure and satisfaction, too, at having won the human to its mysterious purpose — these were colours in the strange picture that Hyde thought of later when dealing with the human herd in his hotel again. At the moment he was aware chiefly of pathos and affection. The whole business was, of course, not to be believed, but that discovery came later, too, when telling it to others.

The digging continued for fully half-an-hour before his labour was rewarded by the discovery of a small whitish object. He picked it up and examined it — the finger-bone of a man. Other discoveries then followed quickly and in quantity. The *cache* was laid bare. He collected nearly the complete skeleton. The skull, however, he found last, and might not have found at all but for the guidance of his strangely alert companion. It lay some few yards away from the central hole now dug, and the wolf stood nuzzling the ground with its nose before Hyde understood that he was meant to dig exactly in that spot for it. Between the beast's very paws his stake struck hard upon it. He scraped the earth from the bone and examined it carefully. It was perfect, save for the fact that some wild animal had gnawed it, the teeth-marks being still plainly, visible. Close beside it lay the rusty iron head of a tomahawk. This and the smallness of the bones confirmed him in his judgement that it was the skeleton not of a white man, but of an Indian.

During the excitement of the discovery of the bones one by one, and finally of the skull, but, more especially, during the period of intense interest while Hyde was examining them, he had paid little, if any, attention to the wolf. He was aware that it sat and watched him, never moving its keen eyes for a single moment from the actual operations, but of sign or movement it made none at all. He knew that it was pleased and satisfied, he knew also that he had now fulfilled its purpose in a great measure. The further intuition that now came to him, derived, he felt positive, from his companion's dumb desire, was perhaps the cream of the entire experience to him. Gathering the bones together in his coat, he carried them, together with the tomahawk, to the foot of the big spruce where the animal had first stopped. His leg actually touched the creature's muzzle as he passed. It turned its head to watch, but did not follow, nor did it move a muscle while he prepared the platform of boughs upon which he then laid the poor worn bones of an Indian who had been killed, doubtless, in sudden attack or ambush, and to whose remains had been denied the last grace of proper tribal burial. He wrapped the bones in bark; he laid the tomahawk beside the skull; he lit the circular fire round the pyre, and the blue smoke rose upward into the clear bright sunshine of the Canadian autumn morning till it was lost among the mighty trees far overhead.

In the moment before actually lighting the little fire he had turned to note what his companion did. It sat five yards away, he saw, gazing intently, and one of its front paws was raised a little from the ground. It made no sign of any kind. He finished the work, becoming so absorbed in it that he had eyes for nothing but the tending and guarding of his careful ceremonial fire. It was only when the platform of boughs collapsed, laying their charred burden gently on the fragrant earth among the soft wood ashes, that he turned again, as though to show the wolf what he had done, and seek, perhaps, some look of satisfaction in its curiously expressive eyes. But the place he searched was empty. The wolf had gone.

He did not see it again; it gave no sign of its presence anywhere; he was not watched. He fished as before, wandered through the bush about his camp, sat smoking round his fire after dark, and slept peacefully in his cosy little tent. He was not disturbed. No howl was ever audible in the distant forest, no twig snapped beneath a stealthy tread, he saw no eyes. The wolf that behaved like a man had gone for ever.

It was the day before he left that Hyde, noticing smoke rising from the shack across the lake, paddled over to exchange a word or two with the Indian, who had evidently now returned. The Redskin came down to meet him as he landed, but it was soon plain that he spoke very little English. He emitted the familiar grunts at first; then bit by bit Hyde stirred his limited vocabulary into action. The net result, however, was slight enough, though it was certainly direct:

'You camp there?' the man asked, pointing to the other side.

'Yes.'

'Wolf come?'

99

'Yes.'

'You see wolf?'

'Yes.'

The Indian stared at him fixedly a moment, a keen, wondering look upon his coppery, creased face.

'You 'fraid wolf?' he asked after a moment's pause.

'No,' replied Hyde truthfully. He knew it was useless to ask questions of his own, though he was eager for information. The other would have told him nothing. It was sheer luck that the man had touched on the subject at all, and Hyde realized that his own best rôle was merely to answer, but to ask no questions. Then, suddenly, the Indian became comparatively voluble. There was awe in his voice and manner.

'Him no wolf. Him big medicine wolf. Him spirit wolf.'

Whereupon he drank the tea the other had brewed for him, closed his lips tightly, and said no more. His outline was discernible on the shore, rigid and motionless, an hour later, when Hyde's canoe turned the corner of the lake three miles away, and landed to make the portages up the first rapid of his homeward stream.

It was Morton who, after some persuasion, supplied further details of what he called the legend. Some hundred years before, the tribe that lived in the territory beyond the lake began their annual medicine-making ceremonies on the big rocky bluff at the northern end; but no medicine could be made. The spirits, declared the chief medicine man, would not answer. They were offended. An investigation followed. It was discovered that a young brave had recently killed a wolf, a thing strictly forbidden, since the wolf was the totem animal of the tribe. To make matters worse, the name of the guilty man was Running Wolf. The offence being unpardonable, the man was cursed and driven from the tribe:

'Go out. Wander alone among the woods, and if we see you we slay you. Your bones shall be scattered in the forest, and your spirit shall not enter the Happy Hunting Grounds till one of

100

another race shall find and bury them.'

'Which meant,' explained Morton laconically, his only comment on the story, 'probably for ever.'

Glossary & Notes

The following word explanations and notes have been added to help the foreign student to gain a better understanding of the text. Each word is explained within its individual context. The number before each word is the line number on the page where the word occurs. Abbreviations: sl. = slang, coll = colloquial, adv = adverb, adj = adjective.

THE TELL-TALE HEART

Page 1

Title There is an English saying to the effect that the heart tells tales that the mouth keeps silent about.

2   **I am mad:** the narrator here is also the hero or villain of the story. And the story takes place inside his mind, exploring his consciousness, his understanding of what is sane and what is mad. What does he think the word 'mad' implies?

3   **not dulled them:** is the narrator thinking madness equals inability to reason?

6   **hearken:** an old-fashioned way of saying listen to me.

6   **how calmly:** notice the switches of mood and opinion — nervous/calmly: disease/healthily — and the claims 'very, very dreadfully nervous': *all* things in heaven etc.

9   **it haunted me day and night:** he doesn't originate ideas, the ideas enter his brain and haunt him. He is, simply, not in control.

13   **. . . with a film over it:** the old man is suffering from glaucoma. Why should his sick eye haunt the mind of the

narrator? Does it remind the narrator of his own sickness, his own distorted view of the world? Is the eye a mirror?

20 **Dissimulation:** hiding the reasons, the motives for action.

20 **was never kinder . . .:** notice the swing, the switch from kindness to murder. This story, and many others like it, are about obsessions that unbalance people.

24 **I put in a dark lantern . . .:** the narrator is himself a dark lantern, a dissimulator whose motives do not shine out.

Page 2

6 **cautiously:** notice the repetition here and elsewhere in the story. Does it show the intensity of the awareness, the thoughts, the scheming of the narrator?

7 **Vulture eye:** a key image. The dark lantern with a thin ray of light and the filmy, vulture eye. This is like a close-up in a film. The parts are standing for the whole.

34 **death watches:** the death watch beetles.

Page 3

5 **terrors that distracted me:** the narrator is creating in the old man the terror he himself has felt.

33 **I knew that sound well too:** the narrator's own heart has beaten with terror.

Page 4

3 **tattoo:** refers here to a rapid beating on a drum.

9 **excited me . . .:** in one sense the murder plan is a battle against the narrator's own nervousness.

30 **scantlings:** beams holding the floor up.

Page 5

8 **deputed:** given authority.

18 **reposed:** lay at rest!

35 **the noise steadily increased:** where is it coming from? The narrator's own heart or his imagination?

EARTH TO EARTH

Page 7

Title When an Englishman is buried in a churchyard, earth is scattered on his coffin and the words 'earth to earth, dust to dust, ashes to ashes' are recited. The title therefore suggests that a funeral or death or something similar is going to take place.

Para 1. The four characters are quickly introduced. The Doctor (the owner of knowledge): the two Hedges (who perhaps want the knowledge the Doctor has): and the observer, the critical observer who is also the narrator.

4 **My little finger says:** the observer feels instinctively that the Doctor is dangerous to know.

10 **picked a friendship:** the usual English is pick a *quarrel*. It is easier perhaps to pick, or to choose, a quarrel rather than a friendship. Elsie chooses to make friends with the Doctor in a quick decisive way.

15 **immersed:** the metaphor here is knowledge equals water. The verb 'immerse' can mean a. to be covered by water as in a baptism and b. to be deeply involved in someone else's ideas. The Hedges are up to their nostrils in the pool of the Doctor's ideas.

18 **compost:** a compost is where organic material (vegetables manure, etc.) is broken down into humus, into a ready food for the soil of a garden. The compost in the story is a symbol. Just as the moon reflects sunlight onto the earth at night, so a symbol reflects meanings from experience into a story. The image of the compost heap is also an image of the dark ideas of the Doctor, as we shall see later in the story.

21 **converted:** the word 'converted' is often used to describe how people are changed from believing in X to believing in Y. To say someone is converted is to say he has taken on a new religious belief.

21   **childless adj.:** The childless couple are barren, are infertile. The compost heap produces fertility. The childless couple are devoted and presumably wanted to have children. The compost heap is thus a substitute, for it ensures a fertile garden.

26   **fierce bacteria:** fierce bacteria break up natural objects. Fierce faith breaks up human conventions. This is one of the basic metaphors in this story.

Page 8

1   **family bible:** notice how the fierce bacteria destroy, break up the *physical object* of the family bible. This is a physical process that is being described. What is the author thereby suggesting?

4   **The 'formula' and the 'oath of secrecy':** show that the Doctor's knowledge is a hidden knowledge, a form of the occult, a magic practice. The 'Mother' suggests that this is a form of fertility worship. Does compost heap equal mother's womb?

15   **Milkwork etc:** wild flowers.

22   **smell of drains:** it is not surprising that a man whose life centres on compost heaps should smell strongly like a drain.

26   **Dr Steinpilz had to leave:** Does Dr Steinpilz's nationality (American German) have any bearing on the story? Is he perhaps like Dr Strangelove, the American German scientist in the film about nuclear war? That is, is he a symbol of dangerous knowledge that can be used for destruction?

31   **esoteric:** books of magical knowledge.

Page 9

15   **fanatic gleam:** the religious belief of Elsie, her fanatic faith, is repeatedly stressed in the story.

17   **. . . premonitory shudder:** The interest of the Hedges in compost heaps has now become a grotesque obsession. At what point does such an obsession become madness? Many occult stories and tales of the macabre, of the grotesque, are

stories of characters who have lost touch with ordinary social reality. They are faces without mirrors. They cannot *see* themselves. They are slaves to an idea. They have no sense of humour, no powers of self-criticism, no feelings of their own failings. How much are they figures of fun? How much are they figures of pity? Why does the narrator have premonitions, dark feelings about the future?

12   **...built an earth-closet:** an outdoor toilet. They do not want to waste their own waste. They have become manure producers.

27   **hay-box cookery:** slow method of cooking by natural heat, much used in wartime.

Page 10

7   **deadbeat coll.:** exhausted.

9   **dead of heart failure:** did he die of heart-failure? How do we know what is true in a narrative?

14   **kith and kin:** family relations.

17   **irreducible:** metal cannot be destroyed by bacteria.

21   **The answer is no . . .:** why does the observer allow them to bury the dead man in a dung heap?

24   **serried:** row after row in lines.

27   **offal from the fish market:** they collected fish guts etc.

30   **relished:** notice how alive and dominant the bacteria have become in this story. Are they the agents of destruction, the soldiers of the microscopic world of warring nature?

33   **summons:** a *call* to attend a court, to be charged with some illegal action.

Page 11

3   **blackout offence:** during the war windows were 'blacked out' at night to stop light from showing, in case enemy planes were overhead.

11   **dig for victory:** a wartime slogan urging people to grow their own food.

THE TRUTH ABOUT PYECRAFT

Title Whose truth?

1   **he sits:** we are in the mind of the narrator as the story is happening.

4   **imploring look:** if Pyecraft is imploring or pleading, then he is in the power of the narrator.

4   **with suspicion:** Pyecraft is worrying that the narrator will use his power in a harmful way.

10   **clubman:** a man who has sufficient wealth not to have to work and who spends most of his time in a club. A clubman is an old-fashioned playboy.

17   **embedded eyes:** Pyecraft is so fat that his eyes lie deep in his fat face, in the bed of his cheeks and brows.

19   **requited:** in the sense of 'pay back' or 'discharge a debt'.

19   **liquid appeal:** in the sense that his eyes are moist and appealing, wet and imploring.

21   **eternally eating:** those who eat a lot are often said to be lonely, unloved people.

Page 13

14   **Hindu great-grandmother:** why is it important to the story to introduce the information that the narrator has a Hindu great-grandmother? What use is the author going to make of this information?

23   **his fatness:** all Pyecraft has is his fatness. He has nobody to share his life with and so he carries his fatness around?

29   **dumpling talk:** a dumpling is made of suet, very fatty and not very nutritious. Dumpling talk is noise without substance.

30   **one stands:** in English, one 'stands up to' punishment as in a boxing ring.

33   **wallowing:** note the critical words used to describe Pyecraft: gross/fat/jelly/great rolling front/wheezed/obese/dumpling /swelled and now wallowing!!

34   **gormandize:** to treat eating like an art-form.

Page 14

6 **to get it down:** his weight.
8 **gonged:** rang the gong for service.
13 **aquarium:** fish with open mouths and lidless eyes in an aquarium, 'stare' in the way Pyecraft stares.

Page 15

11 **immense undertaking:** to poison all that flesh would require a lot of poison!
24 **Loss of Weight:** but how much will the loss be?

Page 16

21 **rattlesnake venom:** magical recipes traditionally consist of items very hard to find.
27 **pariah dog:** stray mongrel.

Page 17

35 **vittles sl.:** 'vitals', i.e. food.

Page 18

24 **cornice:** where the wall meets the ceiling.

Page 19

14 **all over white:** his body was white where it had bumped into the white paint of the ceiling.
21 **Loss of weight — almost complete:** the recipe must have been like an anti-gravity pill!

Page 20

9 **the draught:** here meaning the whole of the potion.

Page 21

1 **euphuism:** elaborate and artificial form of speaking.
12 **shake-up coll.:** temporary bed.
35 **blowfly:** common meat fly — another fat simile.

TIMBER

Page 24

Title 'Timber!' is a cry warning that a tree is about to fall.

3   **patrio-profiteering:** making excessive profit out of the war and pretending to be patriotic at the same time.

9   **encumbered estate:** he has mortgages on his property.

9   **coverts:** woods where good shooting can take place.

17   **. . . embarrassed manner:** A large red-faced clumsy man who looks embarrassed even if he isn't.

Page 25

4   **farewell stroll:** to say goodbye to the 'timber'. Note, he sees the woods as timber, that is, something to be sold.

11   **Deuced sl.:** term that used to be used by military people, etc. It is an emphatic way of saying *very*.

32   **whirring:** the kind of wing-sound made by cock-pheasants.

Page 26

9   **costive:** here meaning late to come into leaf.

7   **straight as the lines of Euclid:** Greek mathematician.

11   **sinister sunset:** the sunset is presumably dark red, the colour of blood, spilt blood, and therefore sinister.

15   **pit props:** the hero's attitude is consistently mercenary.

23   **stuffed group:** his interest in birds is to kill them and stuff their skins!

25   **'the beggars':** this is a milder version of the swearword 'bugger'. Swearwords are often used to indicate that the person swearing has power over what he is swearing about. It's not a question of dislike, it's a question of power.

28   **beaters:** men employed to *beat* the undergrowth so that birds will fly out and the hunters can shoot them for sport.

Page 27

9   **at a good bat:** a slang term in English for speed is 'like a bat

out of hell'.

9 **uncomfortably aware:** the hero does not usually walk in the woods he rides.

23 **it was his wood:** he *owns* the wood, it is his property, and he is in charge.

30 **first sickening little drop:** he is beginning to feel panic in his mind and this is communicating itself to his body, so that his bloodstream is using up more oxygen and suddenly he is short of breath.

Page 28

14 **sighing and threshing:** the laugh of the man, the wind of the woods. What, as it were, are the woods going to do to the man? Notice the technique building up is like that of parallel cutting in a film: we move from the man's action, to the woods' action, to the man's action etc.

Page 29

11 **'nous':** the intelligence, the insight.

20 **scored his knuckles:** the battle between man and wood becomes physically explicit.

28 **half-comatose:** A coma is a kind of sleep, a form of illness in which the body lives but the mind is switched off.

Page 30

1 **fungoid emanations:** the hero's only imaginative vision, only sense of poetry, comes when he is ill.

Page 31

6 **the wind fleered:** it is as if the sleet, the wind and the trees are combining against him.

Page 32

29 **they'll all come down:** the hero realizes he is losing the battle but he is defiant, he has won. The trees will be cut down.

109

THE HOUSE WITH THE BRICK-KILN

Page 34

Title What is going to happen in the brick-kiln?

1 **hamlet:** a small village.

1 **sequestered adv.:** implies hidden away almost secretly.

5 **girt about:** an archaic expression meaning surrounded by.

9 **unoccupied:** a large house in an isolated part of the country is a classic setting for ghost stories, and stories about the macabre in general.

14 **I would sooner look . . .:** The narrator is writing the story in London and looking back, therefore, on the events he is going to describe.

17 **boskage:** woodland.

Page 35

1 **when we left the place:** why did they leave?

25 **meandering:** winding.

Page 36

11 **commensurate:** in the right proportion to.

24 **furred adv.:** certain kinds of limestone get dissolved in water and are deposited in water tanks etc. leaving a *fur* behind.

Page 37

27 **water-colour sketches:** who painted them?

Page 38

8 **. . . smoke:** what is burning?

12 **representation of something:** i.e. a significant, unusual, unexpected event and not part of a routine.

18 **in each of the pictures:** to the painter the brick-kiln is not just a brick-kiln. It is symbolic of something else.

32 **something dreadful:** presumably a ghost or supernatural presence.

35   **Poignancy:** in the sense of sharpness.

Page 39
8   **something had stealthily entered:** the ghost of the painter perhaps?

10   **I felt it then:** why had the narrator not spoken of this before?

25   **'gave me a turn':** implies a shock as if the person had been spun around.

Page 41
1   **qualm:** a feeling of misgiving.

Page 44
2   **right through him:** when is the ghost standing then? Is the time the ghost is moving in and the time Jack is fishing in, the same?

Page 45
28   **it was not Mrs Franklyn:** Is this a picture from the past, a kind of time mirage? Is it the body of the murdered woman that is burning in the brick-kiln?

111

A LONG SPOON

Page 47
Title: 'When you sup (eat) with the Devil, take a long spoon' is an English saying.
Para 1 and 2: the contrast between Stephen (interested in *how* things work) and Dilys (interested in the *quality* of the things produced) is established.

Page 48

1 **give me one good reason:** Dilys is interested in reality, in what actually happens. Stephen is interested in how reality can be changed, in what can be made to happen.

4 **debris:** the mess of bits and pieces left lying on the floor.

6 **gabbeldigook:** the nonsense sounds made by playing the tape backwards.

11 **turned up the volume:** note how Stephen is experimenting with, playing about with, something that really happened. He is *reversing* reality, turning normality back to front. One of the basic rituals of black magic is to do things backwards — say the Lord's prayer backwards, dance in the opposite way in which the earth revolves on its axis, etc.

14 **sonorously:** his voice seems deeper and richer than he expects.

17 **facsimile:** a small-scale *reproduction* of the sound of a steam engine.

18 **stokehole:** where the coal is burnt to give the steam engine its energy. Why does the author use this simile?

27 **the figure:** what has Stephen conjured up?

32 **cravat:** folded linen, worn as a necktie.

Page 49

11 **pontifical air:** the 'devil' speaks with the importance (pontifically) of a bishop!

24 **the Iron Pentacle:** a five-sided figure drawn on the floor, as

part of a black magic ceremony to call up a devil. The Word of Power is the sound recited to help call up the devil.

Page 50

17 **hot clinkers:** hell is often pictured as full of burning stone. A clinker is the stone left over after coal has been burnt. The devil has brought the smell of hell with him.

19 **Old 'Nick':** the Devil.

29 **huffed adv.:** annoyed, and showing it physically. Often used when someone's dignity is upset.

Page 51

1 **I detect no odour of sanctity:** Batruel only expects opposition from priests. He is saying that he does not smell a priest, when he looks at Stephen.

9 **up-to-date coll.:** Batruel is old-fashioned in his dress and the way he is trying to sell the services of the Devil. The implication is that man is doing the Devil's work already and doing it better than the Devil!

Page 52

29 **'Well, I really don't know':** the surprising, comically surprising thing happening is that neither Stephen nor Dilys are very surprised by the Devil being in their sitting-room.

31 **D.P.:** displaced person or refugee.

Page 53

9 **non-existent hilt:** the Devil is used to carrying a sword.

34 **ton:** nineteenth century word for fashion, and fashionable people.

Page 54

21 **Adept:** an expert in magic.

28 **court circles:** mainly aristocratic people, who were often in the company of the King and Queen.

113

Page 55

11 **Bent-Rollsley saloon:** Batruel is confusing the names of the Rolls-Royce and Bentley cars.

Page 56

1 **Debrett:** the book that lists titled people in England.

3 **One must face facts:** Stephen's attitude is that even if he did become wealthy, how would he explain it to the authorities.

23 **Tempter's Manual:** the Bible's Book of Genesis. The serpent tempting Eve (Dilys equals Eve).

Page 57

9 **exorcising:** saying prayers to drive out an evil spirit.

10 **canonized:** to be made a canon — a position in the Church of England.

Page 58

1 **do you play football?:** Stephen wants to win on the football pools. He wants the Devil to arrange for teams to draw.

Page 59

4 **Bentley:** a very expensive car.

17 **Guards:** one of the 'best' regiments socially.

29 **windfall coll.:** here meaning a sudden gift of money.

32 **quibbling:** arguing over small points.

Page 60

15 **braided:** he wore a uniform with braid on it.

34 **dead cert coll.:** an absolutely certain thing.

34 **few bob coll.:** a bob was a shilling in the old British currency.

Page 61

29 **prognostication:** telling the future.

35 **almost without hesitation:** has Gripshaw had experience of this before?

SKIN

Page 63

5 **rue de Rivoli:** a street on the right bank in Paris, renowned for its expensive shops.

21 **plaque:** name plate.

Page 64

11 **refuse can:** containers for rubbish.

25 **tattoo:** a method of injecting ink beneath the skin to form decorative patterns. Traditionally it is favoured by sailors and soldiers.

30 **easel:** a stand for the artist's picture.

Page 65

3 **a great sum of money with my work:** what was Drioli's work?

7 **play hell with coll.:** to be very bad for.

8 **boozy sl.:** tipsy or slightly drunk.

Page 67

20 **gravity:** here meaning a seriousness of mood.

Page 68

17 **on my back:** why does Drioli want the picture on his back? He can't *see* it there!

33 **if anyone knew about the tattoo . . .:** The tattooist explores art as a means of expression and a set of techniques. Drioli wants a painting turned into a tattoo, he wants a body painting based on art not commerce. He wants free, and for himself, and on himself, what he sells to other people.

Page 69

11 **my wife upon my back:** why on his back? Is the picture of his wife meant to protect him? What is the relationship between the boy painter, the tattooist's wife and the tattooist.

115

Page. 72

9 **monstrous centipede:** the wet brush feels like an insect with many legs.

15 **supersede:** take the place of.

31 **small hours:** the hours after midnight.

Page 73

5 **impasto:** method of oil painting with one thick layer on top of another.

Page 75

8 **take yourself out of my gallery:** i.e. art is for the rich and well-dressed.

3 **a flabby face etc:** the speaker is seen as an ugly animal.

15 **a fat white paw:** again the gallery owner is seen as a dog — or low form of life.

20 **flunkey:** an employee in expensive-looking clothes.

Page 76

27 **I will buy it:** Art is a commodity, something to be bought and sold for profit. Art is not the celebration of a struggle to represent life. Art is potential money. The theme of this story: Art minus Life equals Money plus Death.

Page 77

24 **like a farmer:** the theme is becoming very clear. The art dealer sees art as a product to be bought and sold for profit. Art is more important than life, is separated from life.

33 **bask:** a luxurious image — 'basking like a whale' is the usual simile.

35 **chateau of Bordeaux:** the best wines of France.

Page 81

Title: is the wolf running to or away from something?

3 **either a liar or a fool:** this is the central problem of both the mystery story teller and his hero.

9 **supreme loneliness:** the combination of natural beauty and loneliness is the basic mixture, the basic recipe, for many mystery narratives.

11 **singular adj.:** here meaning uncommon, strange.

13 **stiff with fish:** well stocked with fish.

16 **old Indian:** what part is he going to play?

Page 82

7 **portages:** places where rapids make it necessary to carry the canoe up the bank.

13 **primeval wilderness:** the equations — wilderness equals man's unconcious behaviour; wilderness equals man's untamed behaviour — are possible plans for this short story. Certainly, a wilderness is a physical representation of the unknown.

25 **the redskin's god:** only the redskin has lived here, only he has tried to explain why things are as they are: the redskin's god is the redskin's myth, their explanation of order and change.

31 **'made medicine':** made drugs from herbs etc., that expanded their conciousness.

Page 83

18 **kit coll.:** equipment.

26 **'Put yer tent on the east shore':** what is wrong with the west shore?

Page 84

12 **dunnage:** here meaning camping equipment.

15 **less pleasant places:** he cursed them, and their advice.

Page 85

7 **useless hours:** the fish don't rise, when the sun is high.

Page 88

3 **sense of proximity:** feeling of nearness.

28 **original dread:** he had felt terror at being watched by a man, but only man's accustomed superiority when he realised the eyes belonged to an animal.

Page 89

15 **'packed':** starved.

35 **racial visions:** unlike the Indians, he knew nothing about ghost wolves.

Page 91

1 **it courted recognition:** the wolf wants to be recognized as a living being.

6 **nasty customer coll.:** bad enemy, because of its strength.

30 **attendant beast:** what does 'attendant beast' mean in psychological terms? Is it the lonely hunter, or is it an image of the hero himself?

Page 95

20 **windfalls:** the trunks of trees blown down by the wind.

26 **rocky bluff:** cliff projecting into the lake.

Page 98

15 **tomahawk:** the axe of the north American Indian.

25 **great measure:** he had nearly finished his task.

26 **intuition:** immediate, unconcious understanding.

33 **platform of boughs:** the Indians' traditional resting place for the dead.

Page 99

3 **pyre:** bonfire to burn the dead.

118